Healing The Heart Of A Detroit Gangsta

KYIRIS ASHLEY

U.A.D PRESENTS

Stay Up to Date

To stay up to date on new releases, plus get information on contests, sneak peeks and more,

Click the link below...
https://mailchi.mp/6d21003686d1/subscribe

Soundtracks

Scan the QR Code below to listen to the Soundtracks/Singles of some of your favorite U.A.D titles:

Don't have Spotify or Apple Music?
No Sweat!
Visit your choice streaming platform and search URBAN AINT DEAD.

Currently on lock serving a bid?
JPay, iHeartRadio, WHATEVER!
We got you covered.
Simply log into your facility's kiosk or tablet, go to music and search
URBAN AINT DEAD.

U.A.D PRESENTS

Like & Follow us on social media:

FB - URBAN AINT DEAD

IG: @uadpresents

Tik Tok - @uadpresents

Submission Guidelines

Submit the first three chapters of your completed manuscript to urbanaintdead@gmail.com, subject line: Your book's title. The manuscript must be in a .doc file and sent as an attachment. The document should be in Times New Roman, double-spaced, and in size 12 font. Also, provide your synopsis and full contact information. If sending multiple submissions, they must each be in a separate email. Have a story but no way to submit it electronically? You can still submit to URBAN AINT DEAD. Send in the first three chapters, written or typed, of your completed manuscript to:

URBAN AINT DEAD
P.O Box 448
Maybrook, NY 12543

DO NOT send original manuscript. Must be a duplicate.
Provide your synopsis and a cover letter containing your full contact information.
Thanks for considering URBAN AINT DEAD.

PART ONE

The Heartbreak

Chapter One

Reason walked into the dimly lit club, and the sirens sounded, letting all the strippers know there was big money in the building. Reason was a hood celebrity around the city of Detroit with his mother running the top drug organization in Michigan, making Reason both well-known and feared around the metro Detroit area. Every bitch wanted to fuck him, and every nigga wanted to be him. Even though he played around with a few of the bitches, allowing them to taste his dick from time to time, they all knew what was up. Everyone in the city knew about Reason's woman and how long they'd been together.

No matter how much dick he gave them, they all knew it wasn't going any further than that. Reason's heart belonged to one woman, and he planned to keep it that way. Reason, who stood six foot four inches tall with skin that resembled dark chocolate, was what most women would describe as fine as hell. His low-cut Caesar was clean with a fresh lineup and a neatly trimmed beard. Reason was stepping out tonight and was ready to have a good time. He walked to his reserved booth along with the rest of his crew before taking his seat.

The bottle girl, already knowing Reason's order, made her way over to his section with three bottles of Ace of Spades, a bottle of Casamigos, and a bottle of Hennessy. Placing everything on the table, she smiled at Reason as he paid for the drinks. She thanked him, noticing the five-hundred-dollar tip he'd given her. Dancers made their way over to Reason's section, dancing and collecting money, as him and his crew threw it. He knew he was going to pay a few bills that night, and as the song said, it ain't trickin' if you got it.

"These bitches in here thick as fuck. I'm payin' a bitch tuition tonight, maybe even find my next baby mama," Chrome yelled over the music to no one in particular.

Chrome, who stood five foot ten inches tall, was one of the youngest of Reason's crew, only being twenty-one years old. He was skinny, only weighing one hundred forty-five pounds soaking wet. His dark skin and shoulder length locs made him resemble the rapper Lil Wayne. Busting open two of the several packs of singles he had, Chrome tossed them into the air and watched as they rained down on the dancers in front of him.

"What's yo name, baby?" Reason asked one of the dancers that took a seat next to him.

"Bubblegum," she replied, seductively licking her lips.

He looked over at the thick red bone with huge breasts that set up nicely and the thighs that matched. Her long, pink hair was in huge curls which flowed down her back, and her body smelled like candy. She instantly made Reason's dick hard, and he wanted to take her to the back room, so she could give him a private dance.

"Can I get a dance, Bubblegum?" he asked, holding up a stack of money.

Bubblegum smiled, seeing nothing but dollar signs, as she grabbed his hand, leading Reason into the fire and ice room. It was one of the several rooms in the club the dancers could choose from for any of the private services they offered. The rooms were reserved for the big paying costumers only, and Bubblegum knew Reason was one of them. The room was all-white with white walls, fluffy, white, shag carpet, and all-white furniture. The lights in the room, however, changed from blue to red, giving the room a fire and ice feel.

"Have a seat so Bubblegum can take care of you."

Reason took a seat on one of the two couches in the room. He watched as Bubblegum seductively walked over to him, removing the silver pasties and revealing her dark brown nipples. Straddling him, Bubblegum sat on Reason's lap.

"You came in here for a dance, or you want something else?" she whispered, licking the side of his neck. Reason's dick stiffened as he cuffed Bubblegum's soft ass in his hands.

"What else you got in mind, my baby? You let me know what we 'bout to do with our time," he replied, counting out a thousand dollars in blue faced bills before tossing them onto the table.

Sliding down and resting between his legs, Bubblegum placed her mouth against his zipper, using her teeth to unzip his pants. She pulled out his thick manhood and held it inside her hands as she admired it. *Damn, this nigga got a thick ass dick,* she thought as she licked her lips. Opening her mouth, Bubblegum wrapped her lips around his manhood, allowing her saliva to run down his shaft. Reason bit his bottom lip in an effort to prevent the moan that threatened to escape. Bubblegum looked up at him, smiling inside, knowing he was enjoying himself. Bubblegum sucked Reason dry, and when she was done, she was fifteen hundred dollars richer. Reason had counted out five hundred more dollars, placing it on the table, adding to the thousand he'd initially placed there. The head was so good, he thought she deserved more.

"You can come back and see me anytime." Bubblegum winked before walking out the door.

Reason walked out the club with his crew right behind him. It was after two in the morning, and Reason was more than drunk. As he stumbled to the car, his best friend and right-hand asked him for his key fob.

"Ain't no way yo drunk ass 'bout to drive. I'm down with a lot of shit, but drunk driving ain't one of 'em," Ace announced, taking the fob from Reason's hand.

Ace stood six feet two inches tall and two hundred fifty pounds of pure muscle. His low-cut fade, long, full beard, and tattooed body made him a favorite of all the ladies. He had over fifty tattoos, and if there was one thing the ladies loved, it was a big dog with a tattooed frame. Ace knew Reason like the back of his hand and could tell that he was way over his limit. So, there was no way he was allowing him to drive anywhere.

"Nigga, you was drinkin' too," Reason slurred.

"Not nearly as much as you. I had two drinks. I'm good, just get in the car."

Reason got into the passenger seat of his Tesla, and Ace got behind the wheel. Ace pulled off into traffic, leaving the city and heading to the suburban area where they both lived. The night air was cool, and Reason rolled his window down, hoping the air would sober him up a bit before he walked into his house. He hadn't realized how drunk he actually was until he sat down, and his head started spinning. Ace had just merged onto the freeway and got into the middle lane when a car came out of nowhere, hitting them hard and causing them to spin out. The car continued to spin until it crashed headfirst into the viaduct.

Ace woke up several moments later with a pounding headache. He looked around, not knowing what was happening when he realized he was still inside the car. *Shit, we got into an accident,* he thought to himself. Placing his hand on his head, trying to control the pounding, he realized he was bleeding.

"Reason, you good, bro?" Ace asked in concern for his friend.

When Reason didn't reply, he looked over at him to find he was out cold. Reaching into his pants pocket, Ace grabbed his phone and called for help. He prayed that his friend was going to be okay, not wanting anything to happen to him. Reason was covered in broken glass, and blood was gushing from his head. Ace could see the car was crushed on the passenger's side where they'd been hit, leaving Reason compressed in the seat. Several moments later, the ambulance, along with several police cars, arrived on the scene. Ace was able to get out the car on his own and walk over to the ambulance. However, Reason, on the other hand, had to be cut out of the car before being carried to the ambulance.

Once at the hospital, Ace was patched up, only needing a couple of stitches in his forehead. He then placed a call to Reason's mother, letting her know about the accident and telling her the location of the hospital. About fifteen minutes later, Peaches ran inside the waiting room with tears streaming down her face. Ace could tell she was frantic and for good reason. From the look of the accident, he wasn't sure if Reason was even going to make it out the hospital alive.

"Ace, what happened? Did they say how my baby was doing? Oh, my God, I hope he's alright."

"The doctors ain't came out to tell me anything yet. We were in a hit and run on the Southfield Freeway. The shit was bad," he confirmed.

"Y'all went out, didn't y'all? I done told that boy about driving drunk."

"We did go out, but Reason wasn't the one driving. I told him to let me drive because he was too drunk. I was cool and wasn't the cause of the accident. Someone hit us out of nowhere and just kept on going."

Ace shook his head, wishing he could turn back the hands of time. He prayed his best friend would make it through and recover quickly. Opening his arms to Peaches, Ace hugged her tightly as she cried on his chest. She didn't know what to do. Reason was her only son, and it would kill her if anything happened to him. Just as Ace broke their embrace, the doctor walked up to them.

"You are the family of Reason Alexander?"

"Yes, I'm his mother. How is my son doing? Is he going to be okay?"

"We have stabilized him; however, he is not out the woods yet. His left hip was slightly sprained, and there was also some damage to his spinal cord. Right now, he is temporarily paralyzed from the waist down," the doctor informed.

"Oh, my God, paralyzed? Jesus, no, not my baby!" Peaches screamed, almost falling to the floor, and she would have if Ace hadn't caught her.

"This should only be temporary. I am sure with physical therapy, he will make a full recovery," the doctor assured.

"I need to see him."

"Mr. Alexander is still in surgery. Once he is out, you will be able to see him. I can come get you and take you to him at that time."

"Thank you, Doctor," Ace spoke, still holding on to Peaches. He was afraid that if he let her go, she would hit the floor. "Come on, Peaches. Let's sit down while we wait for the doctor," Ace suggested, guiding her to a chair.

They sat there for what seemed like hours before the doctor finally reappeared, informing them both that they could see Reason. Following the doctor, they walked inside the hospital room, and Peaches broke down. Her son was lying there with bandages covering one of his arms and legs. His face was bruised and swollen, and the sight of him broke her heart.

"He is still under the anesthesia; however, once it wears off, he will wake up. Your son really is lucky. If there would have been a break in the spine, he would be paralyzed indefinitely. I will let the two of you have some time with him." The doctor smiled before walking out the room.

"We need to call Kalahni. I forgot to call her when I called you. She don't even know about the accident. She should be here too," Ace suggested.

Peaches just rolled her eyes. She never liked Kalahni from the day Reason introduced them. Peaches could tell a gold-digging ass bitch when she saw one, and that was exactly what Kalahni was. Peaches tried to stay out of their relationship and keep her opinions to herself, knowing that she was who her son chose. However, she knew in her heart that Kalahni wasn't the woman for her son. On the bright side, their relationship did bring Peaches her first grandson, Easton, who she loved dearly. So, it wasn't a total loss.

"You call her because I can't." Peaches looked over to Ace, tears still streaming down her face.

Ace nodded his head, pulling his phone from his pocket and dialing Kalahni's number. The phone rang several times before a sleeping Kalahni finally answered.

"Hey, it's Ace. Reason was involved in a car accident, and he's in the hospital. We think it's best if you come up here."

"Oh, my God, an accident? What hospital?" Kalahni questioned, jumping up out of bed.

"We at Oakwood Main."

"I'm on my way."

Kalahni hung up the phone and slipped into a pair of sweatpants and a T-shirt before grabbing Easton and rushing out the door. She placed a call to her friend, Tori, asking her to look after Easton while she went to the hospital. Without hesitation, Tori agreed, and Kalahni was at her house within fifteen minutes. Her mind was racing a mile a minute, and she prayed that Reason was okay. She pulled into the hospital parking lot and jumped out her car, rushing inside to check on her man.

"Hello, I'm here for my husband, Reason Alexander. He was brought here after being in an accident," Kalahni informed the receptionist as she watched her type his name into her computer. Although

Reason was not technically her husband, she thought the small, white lie would get her to him faster.

"Yes, he is here. He's on the second floor, room 211. Just follow the signs to the elevators and make a left when you get off."

"Thank you." Kalahni smiled before walking down the hall.

She rushed through the halls until she got to the elevator. "Reason, baby, I'm coming. Please be okay," she spoke aloud as she watched the elevator doors close. When she arrived on the second floor, she ran down the hallway until she reached Reason's room. When she entered and saw him lying in the hospital bed, she ran to him, placing her head on his chest as tears ran down her eyes.

"What happened to him?"

"We were in a hit and run on Southfield. We were leaving the club," Ace informed.

"What did the doctors say?"

"He's going to need physical therapy and learn to walk again," Peaches chimed in. She knew Kalahni really didn't care; she could see it in her face. The fake tears that were rolling down her cheeks were just that — fake.

"Walk again? Oh, my God, please tell me this is not happening!"

"Everything gon' be okay, Kalahni. He's alive, and that's the important thing. The hospital is going to set him up with a physical therapist, and before you know it, he's going to be back to normal," Ace assured.

"Yeah, but how long will that take? He's going to need care while he is paralyzed, an at home nurse or something. Who is going to take care of him until he's able to walk again?"

If looks could kill, Peaches would have killed Kalahni twice by the way she looked at her. She couldn't believe the words that had just left her mouth. If she wasn't afraid security would kick her out of the hospital, she would have slapped fire to Kalahni's face.

"What the fuck you mean who's going to take care of him? You live in his home rent free, correct? He's been taking care of you the whole time y'all been together, right? So, what the fuck you mean who's going to take care of him?" Peaches was stunned to say the least.

"I'm going to need help. Easton is already a handful by himself, and he's only two. I'm not going to be able to juggle them both. I've never taken care of a grown man that couldn't walk, so I don't know how to. He's going to need a nurse."

"I understand that you're going to need help, and of course I will help you with my son and grandchild. I also understand this is a lot to take in. It's a lot for us all. None of us expected this to happen. We just gotta work together now," Peaches spoke.

"Peaches is right. It's best that Reason has people around him that care about his wellbeing, not someone that's being paid to do so. I will help too. And between the three of us, we can get it done. It's gon' be okay, Kalahni. You're not going to have to do this alone. We a family, and when shit gets hard, family comes together," Ace assured.

Kalahni looked into the eyes of both Peaches and Ace. Knowing they were being honest softened her heart, and she took a deep breath. She pulled one of the chairs up to Reason's bed and sat next to him. "I just need for him to be okay. I didn't even want him to go out tonight. This never would have happened if he would have just listened to me." Kalahni had her head low as tears fell from her eyes. "Reason, baby, I just need you to get better, baby. Me and our son need you."

Chapter Two

Three weeks had passed, and Reason was finally being released from the hospital. He felt helpless as he sat in his wheelchair, waiting on his mother to walk back inside the room. He was still trying to adjust to not being able to walk. Although temporary, he couldn't help but to feel like an invalid. He sat there, looking down at legs that he used to take for granted. You never knew how much you needed something until it went away. Something as simple as getting out of bed and walking to the bathroom was now something Reason wasn't able to do.

How the fuck is any of them niggas gon' take me seriously and I'm sittin' in a fuckin' wheelchair?

"Are you ready to go home?" Peaches asked, walking back into the hospital room a few moments later.

"Yeah, I'm sick of this place. I been here too long."

Peaches nodded her head and walked over to Reason. She pulled the brake lever back on the wheelchair and began wheeling him outside. She had to get two male nurses to help her place him inside the car because there was no way Peaches' small frame could lift him. This only added to Reason's frustration. He couldn't wait to start physical therapy and get better, so this would all be over. There was no way he could allow his family to have the burden of taking care of him. He vowed then to do everything he could to make sure this wouldn't last long.

Peaches pulled up to Reason's home, and both Ace and Kalahni were waiting on him there. They helped him out the car and into the wheelchair Kalahni had picked up for him. Peaches had a wheelchair ramp connected to Reason's front porch to make it easier for him to get in and out the house along with other handicap accessible items Reason would need around the house.

"Baby, I'm so happy you're home. Easton couldn't wait to see you. He's been asking since he woke up this morning what time you would be coming home," Kalahni revealed.

"I missed my little man too. Let me get in here so I can see him." Reason began wheeling himself up the ramp. When he got to the door, he tried to lean forward to open it but couldn't reach the knob. Instinctively, Peaches rushed over to him and opened the door for him, bruising Reason's ego without even realizing. He wheeled himself inside the house with the rest of them following behind.

Easton, who was already sitting on the couch, jumped up and ran over to Reason. His little legs were moving as fast as they could. "Daddy, I missed you so much. You was gone for a looong time. Mommy said you was sick. Are you better? And what is that?" Easton questioned, pointing down at Reason's wheelchair. Kalahni hadn't explained anything to Easton, mainly because she didn't know how to. How could someone tell a two-year-old that their daddy couldn't walk and wouldn't be able to do most of the things they did together before the accident?

"It's my wheelchair. These wheels gon' be my new legs for a while until Daddy can walk again. And yeah, Daddy's feeling a lot better, lil man."

"It looks fun. Can I do it?"

Reason held out his arms and picked Easton up, putting him on his lap. He wheeled him around the house several times as Easton cheered. Reason had missed his son so much and was grateful to be back home. He knew he had a long road ahead of him but was ready to take it on. He vowed to himself that he would do all he could to ensure he wouldn't be in this wheelchair for long.

"Are you hungry, baby? I got some takeout from that Mexican restaurant you like," Kalahni offered.

"Yeah, that sounds good as hell."

"I'll be right back." Kalahni headed over to the kitchen to fix Reason a plate.

"Can I get you anything else, bro?" Ace asked.

"Nah, I'm as good as I can be. I do need to talk to you though. Let's go…" Reason stopped, looking down at his legs, realizing he couldn't walk down the basement stairs and into his office. He bit his bottom lip as he shook his head. Something as simple as walking down the stairs was something that he couldn't do. His manhood felt nonexistent. *How the fuck can I protect my family if I can't even walk up and down the steps? I gotta get this shit together.*

"Here you go, baby." Kalahni walked back into the living room, interrupting Reason's thoughts.

"Thank you, boo. Can you take Easton upstairs while I talk to Ace?"

Kalahni nodded her head and scooped Easton into her arms before heading upstairs. Reason looked over to Peaches, who was still sitting on the couch. She nodded her head, taking the hint, and walked outside to smoke a cigarette. Once Reason was sure everyone was out of earshot, he began to speak.

"How did that hit go on Kilo? Did we see that through?"

"After the accident, I sent Chrome to handle Kilo. Thing about it was, he hit his twin brother, Brick, not knowing. I just found out a couple days ago that Kilo is still breathin'. That nigga hidin' out though. He already know what's up. We gon' get that nigga though."

Kilo used to be Reason's little homie until he thought it was wise to rob two of Reason's spots. Reason had taken Kilo under his wing and showed him the game, so he could get it on his own. Unfortunately, Kilo didn't want to work for his and thought it better to take it. Reason heard the streets talking about Kilo hitting different spots, but he would have never thought his would be one of them. However, when Reason got the call that two of his spots had been hit in the same night, he knew exactly who was to blame. Reason was known in the streets as the nigga not to fuck with. So, as much as it would pain him to do so, he had no other choice but to put Kilo down permanently.

"Yeah, we gotta get that nigga. Ain't no way niggas in the hood 'bout to think it's okay to play with me. Wheelchair or not, I'll still put two in they head."

"I got you, my G. Don't even worry 'bout it. All you should be worried about is getting better. I can handle the business til then," Ace assured.

Ace was Reason's best friend since the third grade. They grew up together like brothers with their mothers even forming a friendship until Ace's mother died of breast cancer in his senior year of high school. Besides his mother, Ace was the only other person Reason totally trusted. With Ace being his right-hand man, Reason knew he could trust Ace to make sure Kilo was handled.

"I know you got it, just make sure you keep me in the loop."

"You already know," Ace agreed before slapping hands with Reason. "I'm about to head out but call me if you need anything," Ace continued before heading out the door.

Peaches walked back into the house, joining Reason in the living room. "You want me to stay tonight and help you?"

"Nah, Ma, Kalahni got me. I'ma be good."

Peaches rolled her eyes, not trusting Kalahni to take care of her son. Reason was her only child, so she needed to ensure he was taken care of properly. She wasn't sure if Kalahni was capable of doing so.

"Come on, Ma. Why you rollin' yo eyes? Kalahni is going to be my wife. We been together for the past five years, and we building a family. She not going nowhere, and it's time that you accepted that."

"I don't have to accept shit. I tolerate that bitch because she's my grandchild's mother. But I don't like that bitch nor do I trust her. I'm telling you now, Reason, don't put that bitch name on nothing just cause you in that damn wheelchair. You give that bitch access to yo accounts, and she gon' rob you blind. That's the type of bitch she is. She might can fool you, but that ho ain't foolin' me," Peaches barked.

"Ma, stop. You will not stand in our house and disrespect Kalahni. I understand that you have your own opinions of her, but they are yo opinions. Keep that shit to yourself, especially when you standing in this house. You know I love you, Ma, but I have to draw the line."

Peaches, not believing her son was taking anyone's side over her, especially a no-good bitch like Kalahni, now felt hurt. Peaches was lost for words, which was rare for her. With that, she nodded her head, grabbed her purse, and walked out the door.

Over the next few days, Reason tried to adapt to his new normal. Although he was still getting used to Kalahni bathing him, he was able to get up and down the stairs himself by using the lift chair Ace had installed. Peaches had called to set up his physical therapy, which was due to start in a couple of weeks. He was sitting on the couch with Easton next to him as they watched Easton's favorite episode of *Spider-Man*. He enjoyed the quality time he was able to spend with his son; he just wished it was under different circumstances.

"Come on, Easton, let's put your shoes on, so we can go," Kalahni called out before entering the living room. She was dressed in a black Chanel one piece, which was so tight it looked painted on. The gold Fendi jewelry set she wore looked good against the black fabric. The forty-inch, six thirteen bust down she rocked hung past her butt with every hair in place. Her red lips looked juicy and kissable, and her Angel Share perfume entered the room before she did.

"Where you going lookin' like you lookin'?" Reason joked, looking over at her.

Kalahni sat on the couch next to Easton, placing his feet into his blue and white Dunks before answering. "I'm going out for drinks with Tori, and I'm taking Easton to my mama's house."

"Why you taking him over yo mama's house? He can stay right here with me," Reason suggested, smiling down at Easton.

Kalahni rolled her eyes, not even looking up to Reason. Once Easton had his shoes on, she placed his arms into his jacket and took his hand into hers. "Tell Daddy you will see him tomorrow."

"Tomorrow? Come on, Kalahni, why you taking him to yo mom's? She don't even like watching kids. He can stay right here with me and chill at home."

"And how the fuck are you supposed to take care of him if you can't even take care of yourself? You roll around here in your wheelchair, needing everyone to help you do everything. You can't even go to the bathroom yourself, and you want me to leave my son with you while I go out? You must be fuckin' crazy. He going to my mother's house!" Kalahni spat. "You can't even fuck me. You would think that with yo dick not working, you would be eating this pussy right. I told you I would even sit on yo face last night. All you had to do was lay there, and yo ass act like you couldn't even do that shit!" Without waiting for a response, Kalahni scooped Easton into her arms and walked out the door, leaving Reason sitting in his wheelchair stunned.

"Damn, way to tell me how you really feel," Reason spoke aloud once Kalahni closed the door. His feelings were crushed by her words, and his ego was bruised. He would have never thought Kalahni would say such hurtful words to him. He knew Kalahni was frustrated with the way things were going, but she was supposed to be there for him. They were supposed to be life partners. If the roles were reversed, Reason would be by Kalahni's side day and night without question. Now, there Kalahni was, leaving him alone.

Damn, this how she really gon' do me? How would she be acting if we were married? Or if this shit wasn't just temporary? Reason would have given his life for Kalahni, now there she was, treating him like she didn't care at all.

Kalahni dropped Easton off and headed right to Starters. She couldn't wait to get a few lemon drops in her system. Her home life had been extremely stressful to say the least. She was in dire need of a lady's night, and when she got Tori's call, she got dressed immediately.

Walking into the restaurant, Kalahni instantly spotted Tori sitting at a table. Letting the hostess know she was joining her friend, Kalahni walked over to the table. "Hey, girl, you over here lookin' like a whole snack," Kalahni greeted Tori.

Tori was a few inches shorter than Kalahni, standing only about four foot eleven inches. Her chocolate skin was smooth and without blemishes. Her natural brown hair was parted down the middle and hung halfway down her back. The tan colored Gucci two piece she wore looked good on her and showed off all of her curves.

"Thank you, bitch. Yo ass lookin' good too."

The two friends hugged before taking their seats at the table. The waitress walked over, and they both placed their drink orders and looked over the menu as they waited for their drinks.

"So, what's up, girl? How you holdin' up over there with that newly crippled nigga?"

"Girl, this shit is a fucking nightmare. He needs me for every fucking thing. He can't even take a shit without needing me to help. His dick don't work either, girl. This shit is too fucking much."

"Of course his shit don't work, bitch. The nigga paralyzed. I know he eating that pussy though. Just enjoy not having to do no work and still get yours. Shit, I know I would," Tori spoke.

"Bitch, he ain't did that shit either. If I had balls, them bitches would be blue. To go from fuckin' damn near every day to absolutely nothing is insane."

"Give him some time, Kalahni. He's recovering from a traumatic experience. And on some real shit, it can't be easy for him to need you for everything now. I'm sure sex is the last thing on his mind."

"Yeah, and I don't know how long I can deal with this shit."

"Bitch, go get you a rose and calm the fuck down. You gonna be okay." Both women laughed before Kalahni changed the subject.

"So, what's been up with you? What's new in yo life?"

"Shit, you know me. Still getting these niggas for they money, so I can be kicked up and comfortable. But it is this one nigga that I'm starting to like a little bit."

"Awe, shit, I know you fuckin' lyin'. I can't remember the last time I heard you talking 'bout likin' a nigga. I need all the details. Who is he, and how did you meet him?"

"Well, I met him at the club I work at. We not serious or nothing, but I do like him. I'ma keep it to myself for now, but if we get serious, I'll let you know who he is."

"Okay wit' yo secretive ass. I see you," Kalahni joked. The two women sat and had drinks for hours before both left the restaurant, going their separate ways.

Chapter Three

Peaches sat in her living room with stacks of money across her coffee table. She'd just come from picking up the money from her different dope houses across the city. That was usually Reason's job, but she'd taken over since the accident. Peaches had been in the drug game for the last twenty years and was at the top of the food chain, having been the top supplier in Michigan for the past two decades. Known in the streets as DP, short for Dope Girl P, Peaches was nothing to be played with. She'd planned on making her exit from the game, leaving the family business to her son and only child. However, when Reason got into his accident, she knew she would need to wait until he fully recovered before doing so. With people still depending on the drugs she sold, she knew she would have to hold down their organization until Reason was able to take over.

Hearing a knock at her door, Peaches got up to answer it. Looking out of the peephole and seeing it was Ace, Peaches smiled before opening the door.

"What yo sexy ass in here doing?" Ace asked, walking into Peaches' front door and wrapping his arms around her. He pulled her in and kissed her passionately.

"Shit, I'm just in here 'bout to count this money up. I had to go by all the spots today."

"Yeah, and you been working hard as hell today, I see. I don't know why you didn't call me to do that shit for you. You are past the point of getting yo hands dirty. I told you I could handle the business until Reason gets better."

"And I told you no. What I look like handing over a business to my son's friend?"

"It would look like you handing a business over to yo man that already works with the company." Ace wrapped his hands around Peaches' perfectly proportioned hips before kissing her lips softly. "Baby, it's no reason for you to be still doing this shit. I'm here to make your life easier. I'm yo man, and I'm here to help you. So, let me help you."

Peaches and Ace had been in a secret relationship for the past year. It all started after she had a flat tire one night and was stuck on the side of the road. With Reason being out of town, Ace was the one to come and help her. He followed her back to her house, ensuring her safety, and she allowed him to come inside for a drink. From that day forward, they couldn't get enough of each other. She loved spending time with Ace, but she loved fucking him even more. At forty-eight years old, Peaches felt she was in her prime. So, the stamina of a younger man was exactly what she needed. As much as she cared about Ace, she couldn't take her relationship with him as seriously as she wanted, knowing that her son would disapprove. However, she was going to allow him to dick her down for as long as they could keep things a secret.

"Ace, you know damn well I can't do that. I don't even want Reason to know we have anything going on. You're already Reason's right-hand. So, when he takes over the company, you will be the second in command," Peaches spoke.

Ace nodded his head in agreement, although he didn't like what he was hearing. He wanted full control of Peaches' company and thought because he was fucking her, he should be next in line. *I ain't givin' her old ass this good ass dick for nothing. Reason can't even walk. How the fuck is he gonna run an entire drug organization? He can't do his part of the business now,* Ace thought to himself. He wanted to tell Peaches just that, but instead, he kissed her and walked over to the couch before taking a seat.

"I just know you been wanting to get out the game for a minute now. I just want to help you with that, baby. I love you, and I just want the best for you, my baby. That's all."

"I know, and that's sweet. I love you too. But this is my business, and when I step down, my son will be the only one that takes my place."

Ace nodded his head. "You need some help with this?" he asked, quickly changing the subject and pointing to the stacks of money on the table.

"Yeah, I'm not trying to be doing this shit all night."

With that, Ace picked up one of the stacks and began counting. He knew it had to be about a million dollars in cash in front of him, and that was all the more reason why he needed to take over the organization. He made good money as Reason's right-hand, but he could create generational wealth if he was able to run the organization. *I gotta apply more pressure to Peaches. This bitch gon' hand over this organization one way or another.*

Several hours later, they were all done counting, and now, Peaches was ready to get into something else. Standing to her feet, she walked into her kitchen and grabbed the bottle of tequila from her kitchen counter. Peaches then motioned for Ace to follow her to her bedroom. Pulling her shirt over her head, Peaches exposed the perky double D breasts that her doctor had lifted perfectly. She slowly walked over to Ace, who'd taken a seat on her bed. She pulled the top off the tequila and put the bottle to her lips, allowing the liquor to run down her throat before handing the bottle to Ace. Peaches got on her knees in front of Ace and pulled his manhood out. Putting it into her mouth, she sucked until she heard the moans that escaped his lips.

She stood to her feet, removing her sweatpants, before easing herself down onto Ace's manhood, her wetness curving to fit his rod inside her. She moaned as she moved her hips slowly. Ace grabbed her round ass, cupping it in his hands as he guided her movements. She kissed his neck softly as she picked up speed, causing Ace to moan louder.

"Damn, this shit feels so good, baby. You gon' have to slow down before you make me cum in this pussy. We can't be makin' no babies," Ace warned.

With that, Peaches jumped up from his lap, getting on all fours on her bed as Ace stood to his feet. She knew Ace liked hitting it doggy style, and she was going to allow him to give her as many back shots as his heart desired. Grabbing both of Peaches' hips, Ace entered her again.

"Yessssssss, Ace! Fuck this pussy good, Daddy," she screamed out.

I know this bitch ain't calling me 'Daddy', and she old enough to be my fuckin' mama. Let me just hurry up and get this damn nut, so I can go, Ace thought to himself. He never meant to take things this far with Peaches. She caught him one night when he was drunk, and he allowed her to give him a little head. That was all it was supposed to be until he realized he stood to gain a lot from Peaches as long as he was dicking her down as much as she wanted. He just hoped he could give her enough dick to lure her into turning her organization over to him instead of Reason. He knew Reason was her only child, but he also knew women would do anything for a man with good dick.

"That's right, baby. Take this dick Daddy giving you. Take all this shit," Ace coached as he pounded deeper and harder. Peaches couldn't take anymore as her body started to shake uncontrollably, letting Ace know that she'd reached her climax. He began to moan loudly, forcing his orgasm to come. When he finished, he went straight to the bathroom to wash himself. Once fully dressed, he walked back into Peaches' room and took a seat on her bed.

"What you got up for the rest of the night?" Peaches asked.

"Shit, I got some business to take care of," he replied.

"Damn, so I guess you can't stay, huh?"

"Not tonight, baby, but I promise I'll spend the night soon."

Peaches nodded her head before kissing Ace on the lips. She walked him to the door and watched him until his car pulled out of her driveway. *Damn, that man fine as hell and got good dick. I'ma fuck around and fall in love for real,* Peaches though to herself as she locked her door. She fell asleep that night with thoughts of Ace running through her mind.

Kalahni had just finished helping Reason get dressed, and he was sitting in the living room waiting on Peaches. It was his first day of physical therapy, and as nervous as he was about going, he knew this was the only thing that would help him walk again. He knew Kalahni was getting tired of waiting on him hand and foot. That was something she showed to him every day. Although Reason tried to do everything he could on his own, he still found himself needing Kalahni for a lot. She bathed him, helped him to the bathroom, got him dressed, as well as in and out of bed, on top of cooking and cleaning the house and taking care of their son. Reason was starting to feel more like a dependent of Kalahni's than her man. He could feel the change in her attitude toward him since the accident.

It hurt him to see the change because Reason would have bet money that Kalahni would ride out with him through anything. However, this was just becoming too much for her. He knew that once he was able to walk again, things would go back to normal, and he couldn't wait for that day to come.

Several moments later, Peaches was walking through the door ready to take Reason to his appointment. "You ready, son? Today is the first day of the rest of your life. This is gonna make you better, and before you know it, you gonna be back to normal."

"I ain't gonna lie, Ma. I'm a little nervous. What if this shit don't work, and I'm stuck in this chair forever?" This was the first time Reason was speaking his fears aloud to anyone, and they had been weighing on him heavily.

"It's going to work. The doctor already said this was only temporary. This physical therapy is exactly what you need, Reason. Don't overthink things and allow fear to discourage you. You gonna be walking around here running shit before you know it."

"Thanks, Ma. I needed that." Reason smiled.

"You know I got you. You ready to go?"

"Yeah, let's get it."

Reason and Peaches arrived at his physical therapy appointment fifteen minutes early, and Peaches parked out front and went inside, leaving Reason in the car. She returned a few moments later with two male nurses. They helped Reason out the car and into his wheelchair before Peaches wheeled him inside the building.

"I'm gonna go sign you in. I'll be right back," Peaches informed before walking up to the desk. A few moments later, Reason was being called into the back. He was wheeled into a room that resembled a small gym. There was different exercise equipment, such as treadmills, weights, and bars. He looked around, wondering how the process actually worked. Several moments later, a tall, muscular white man that looked to be in his late twenties walked into the room.

"Hello, Mr. Alexander. I'm your PT's assistant, Shane. I just have a couple of questions to ask you before Serenity comes in to start your session. The hospital has already faxed over your chart, and we're aware of your accident, but has there been any change in your diagnoses? For instance, have you regained any feeling in your legs?"

"Nah, everything is still the same."

"Okay, no worries. Most people in your condition don't see results until after the first six months. So, that's normal. Are you on any other medications besides the ones prescribed to you by your doctor at the time of the accident?"

"No," Reason answered.

"Okay, good. Now, do you have any questions for me?" Shane asked, looking up from Reason's chart.

"You said most people don't see results within the first six months. How long does it normally take for people who are temporarily paralyzed to start walking again?"

"Well, that I can't say because everyone's situation is different. However, I can say Serenity is one of the best PTs in the state of Michigan. So, you are in the best hands possible. Serenity will do everything she can to ensure you fully recover."

Reason nodded his head, having no other questions. With that, Shane got up from his seat, letting Reason know that Serenity would be in shortly. Reason hoped he would be one of the few people to show results quickly. He was tired of being confined to a wheelchair and was ready to walk again. He felt less of a man in his everyday life and felt his legs were the key to his manhood.

"Hello, Mr. Alexander, my name is Serenity, and I'm your PT."

Reason looked up at the beautiful, caramel complected woman that walked into the room. Reason thought she would be dressed in a more professional outfit, possibly some scrubs and a white coat. However, Serenity was dressed in a tight fitted, two-piece, yoga pants set, which showed off every curve she possessed. Reason took one look at her and knew her body was all natural, given to her by God and kept up by the gym. He smiled at her as she walked over to him and shook his hand.

"It's nice to meet you. But call me Reason. That Mr. Alexander shit is too formal."

Serenity smiled, taking her seat in the chair across from Reason. "Okay, Reason it is then. I see that you have been in your wheelchair for a little over a month. Don't worry. We gon' get you right, and you'll be walking again in no time. I follow my own routine of physical therapy that worked for most of my patients with over ninety-five percent of them making a full recovery. Although some of my techniques might not be ideal medically, I stand on my holistic therapy treatments, and I feel this would work for you. However, if you are against the holistic treatments, we can go with regular physical therapy. I like to give my patients a choice of treatment."

"If the holistic physical therapy is your best treatment, then that's the one I want. I want nothing more than to be out of this wheelchair and back on my feet."

"I got you, Reason. We got this," Serenity stated, pointing one neatly manicured finger toward the both of them.

Reason nodded his head as he looked into her eyes. For some reason, he trusted her and believed her treatment would work. Her eyes showed honesty, and that was something that Reason valued. He felt in his soul that if anyone could help him walk again, it would be Serenity, and he was happy that she was chosen to be his physical therapist.

Serenity walked out the room, informing Reason she would be back momentarily with Shane. She let him know she would need his help during the therapy session. She returned a few moments later with Shane right behind her. Serenity walked over to a white cabinet in the far corner of the room. She pulled out several white bottles before walking back over to Reason.

"Shane, if you could get him out of the chair and onto the mat. Be sure to remove his shoes and socks."

"No problem, Serenity."

Shane wheeled Reason over to the long, black, floormat, helping him out the chair and down to the floor. "Lean back on your arms," Shane spoke. Reason followed his directions. Once Shane had removed his socks and shoes, Serenity made her way over to him. She got down on the floor before scooting in front of him.

"I will start off each session with a massage with a few of my oils, enriched with herbs and vitamins, which will promote healthy blood flow." Serenity poured some of the oil into her hands before rubbing it onto Reason's legs and feet as she let him know all the benefits of the oils.

"Now, we will start off with a few leg exercises. You let me now if it becomes too much for you, and we can take a break."

Reason agreed, and Serenity began elevating Reason's legs one by one. She did that several times before placing five-pound weights on each one of his ankles, making sure she kept him informed in everything she did. When the hour-long session was over, Shane helped Reason back into his wheelchair. Serenity handed him a box of herbal tea that she told him to drink every night before bed. They also set up appointments for three times a week before Shane wheeled him back into the waiting area where Peaches waited. The same two male nurses helped Reason back into the car.

Reason felt better than he'd felt since the accident. In the short hour-long session with Serenity, he'd gained hope. Something about the way that she made direct eye contact when she spoke to him let him know that she believed in every word she said. The confidence she had in her work gave him the confidence he needed for recovery. He vowed to himself then that he would put in all the work. No matter how hard it got or how tired he was, he wouldn't quit. He would work hard until it paid off.

When Peaches pulled back into Reason's driveway, Ace was getting out of his car. "Damn, a nigga got good timing. I was coming to see how your physical therapy session went." Ace smiled, opening Peaches' passenger side door. He waited for Peaches to wheel Reason's chair over to him before helping him get out the car.

"It was cool. My PT's name is Serenity, and she is using a holistic therapy method on me. She says she thinks that would work the best for me."

"I don't know about this shit. You need real therapy, Reason. I don't know what that holistic shit even means. It all just sounds like some voodoo shit to me. She bust out some crystals, and we getting the fuck up outta there," Peaches announced, only halfway joking.

"Nah, Ma, she really believes in her work, and I fuck with that. She says it won't take me long to be able to walk again with her technique.

She's one of the best in the business anyway, so going somewhere else ain't gon' do shit."

Kalahni was sitting on the couch, scrolling Netflix, when Ace walked in with Peaches and Reason. She was enjoying her peace and quiet with Easton asleep and Reason gone. Taking care of Reason was becoming too much for her. *This was not what the fuck I signed up for. I was only with this nigga because of the money he made and who he was in the damn streets. He ain't nobody if he gon' stay in this fuckin' wheelchair. I'm sick of doing everything for that helpless ass nigga.* Kalahni rolled her eyes and got up from the couch, greeting Reason as he was rolled inside.

"Hey, baby, how was therapy?"

"It went good. She's certain I'll make a full recovery."

"That's good. I'm happy to hear that. Do you know what you want for dinner? I want to start cooking early. I'm a little hungry."

"You don't have to cook, baby. We can order out tonight. Maybe watch a movie or something?" Reason suggested.

"Yeah, that's cool. Just let me know what you want, and I'll order it on Door Dash."

"I'm about to get up outta here. I got something to take care of, but I'll call and check on you tomorrow. And I'll be here Wednesday morning to take you to therapy," Peaches assured before walking out the door.

"I was gon' chill with y'all, but I see y'all trying to have a date night, so I'ma roll out. But I'll be over tomorrow to talk to you," Ace spoke, feeling like the third wheel.

"We can talk now. Kalahni can go in the other room if you got some information for me?" Reason questioned, referring to the hit they had out on Kilo. Reason was hoping Ace was about to tell him he was cold and ready to be put in the ground.

"Nah, it ain't nothing like that. I wanted to talk to you about some whole other shit. It can wait til tomorrow though. Y'all have a good time," Ace assured before walking out the door.

Peaches was still sitting in her car when Ace walked outside. She rolled her window down, getting his attention, and he walked over to her car. She asked him to follow her home, letting Ace know that she missed him. With a smile, Ace obliged and got into his car, pulling off right after Peaches.

Kalahni put in an order from Outback Steakhouse because Reason wanted a steak. By the time the food arrived, Easton was awake from his nap. Kalahni made their plates, and they all sat in the living room, watching a movie while they ate. For those few hours, it felt like everything was normal again. They sat there as a family, enjoying food and movies. They were about three movies in and were sharing more laughs than they had in weeks. That was until Reason asked Kalahni to help him to the bathroom. Blowing out a loud breath of frustration, Kalahni stood to her feet and waited for Reason to roll himself to the bathroom.

"I got something for you once Easton goes to sleep for the night," Reason assured. He was feeling great after his therapy session and was feeling up to giving Kalahni exactly what she wanted.

Kalahni smiled, not knowing what Reason was referring to, but she was more than ready to find out. Reason had been known for giving Kalahni lavish gifts such as cars, diamonds, and purses. So, she could only imagine what he had in store for her next. With her spirits brighter at the thought of the gift she was about to receive, she suddenly didn't mind helping Reason to the bathroom. Once they made it back into the living room, they were able to watch one more movie before little Easton got so sleepy he couldn't keep his eyes open.

"I'm gonna put him to sleep, and I'll be right back," Kalahni stated, picking Easton up into her arms and taking him up to his room. She was eager to see what Reason had for her as she rushed to put Easton to sleep. Once he was tucked into bed, she rushed back down the stairs, ready to receive her gift.

"Okay, baby, I'm ready," Kalahni called out as she rushed back into the living room.

Reason smiled, seeing the huge smile on her face. He rolled his wheelchair as close to the couch as he could get it before leaning over, placing both hands firmly on the couch. Pushing down, he lifted himself out of the chair before turning over and sitting on the couch. Kalahni looked at him, not knowing what was coming next. She watched as he picked both his legs up on the couch before scooting down and lying flat on his back.

"Take your clothes off," he ordered.

Kalahni stood there for a few seconds before walking over to him. She obliged, taking off her light blue joggers, revealing the fact she wasn't wearing any panties underneath. She pulled her white tank over her head, and Reason looked at her, admiring her naked body.

"Come sit on my face, so Daddy can eat that pussy. I ain't tasted it in a while, and I been missin' it," Reason spoke, licking his lips.

Kalahni instantly moistened. It had been a couple months since Reason had so much as touched her, and she was eager to feel him. Although making love was something she knew Reason couldn't do, she was happy enough with the oral services he was offering. Placing her leg over his shoulder, she straddled his face as she eased down on his wet tongue. She moaned loudly as his tongue flickered on her love button, causing her juices to flow into his mouth.

"Yes, Daddy, eat this pussy. You know I need this shit," Kalahni called out, grabbing Reason's head and pushing it deeper into her wetness. She screamed out even louder when Reason lifted his hand and inserted two fingers inside her. She rode his fingers and face at the same pace once she felt her orgasm approaching, screaming out in ecstasy when her body erupted and breathing heavy like they had just made real love. She smiled, feeling completely satisfied, as she helped Reason back into his wheelchair.

"Can you go make my tea? It's on the kitchen counter. I have to drink a cup every night before bed."

"I got you, baby. I'll be right back," Kalahni assured, making her way to the kitchen.

Chapter Four

Ace laid in bed with Peaches asleep next to him. He knew the grade A dick he'd just put on her had put her to bed. He wanted to do everything he could to make Peaches change her mind about handing her organization over to him while Reason was healing. He thought that if he gave her enough good sex, she wouldn't be able to continue to tell him no. His plan was to be the biggest drug kingpin Detroit had ever seen. He just knew he needed Peaches' organization to do so. *I'ma keep dickin' her down for a couple more weeks, then I'll bring it back up to her. She gotta break at some point, and when she does, I'ma fuck the city up. It's my turn to be at the top, and this is just the thing to do it.*

Ace wanted to leave and go home but knew he would have to apply pressure if he wanted his plan to work. He knew he would have to make Peaches think she was his one and only. That was his only way to ensure his plan worked. With that, Ace rolled over and pulled Peaches close to him, holding her tightly the remainder of the night.

The next morning, Ace woke up and drove to Coney Island to pick up breakfast before Peaches woke up. He placed her food onto a plate before adding the plate to a wood tray with a glass of apple juice and carrying it into Peaches' room. He woke her softly, and she smiled when she realized Ace was serving her breakfast in bed.

"Damn, I get all of this?" she asked, biting into a sausage link.

"This ain't shit, just wait until you see the day I have planned for us." Ace smiled.

"Oh, you planning out my days now?" Peaches asked, cutting her eyes at him.

"Damn, I can't plan a date with my woman? Y'all women always talkin' 'bout niggas don't be romantic and shit. Well, this is me tryin' to be romantic."

"Ace, I never told you I wanted you to take me out anywhere. You know we can't be seen in public. If Reason found out about this shit, do you know how mad he would be?"

"You can't hide our love forever, Peaches. You are a grown woman. I don't know why you worried about what he thinks anyway. You make me happy, and I thought I made you happy. You telling me I can't even plan a date with my woman?"

"You do make me happy, Ace," Peaches said, scooting up in her bed to be closer to him. She placed her hand onto his before she continued. "This is why I don't want Reason or anyone else to find out about us. Keeping our love a secret is the only way I know for sure it will be protected. The moment that Reason finds out about us, this will have to end, and I don't want that. I'm not ready to give you up yet, so I need for us to remain a secret."

"I'm not asking you to shout from the mountaintop that we fuckin'. I just simply want to enjoy the day with you. You didn't even ask what I had planned. You think I don't know we on the low? I been knowin' that shit since day one. So don't you think I know to go to discreet places?"

Peaches, now feeling bad for not hearing him out first, smiled at him before apologizing. "You're right, and I shouldn't have just jumped to conclusions like that. We can go do everything you planned for us to do. I would love to spend the day with you, Ace."

And there it go. Just like that, I got her ass. And this was easier than I thought it would be, Ace thought to himself, knowing that if she would allow him to persuade her to go out in public then this was just the start of the long list he had. His charm and charismatic energy was doing a number on Peaches, and soon she wouldn't be able to resist Ace. Or at least that was what he thought.

Once they were finished eating breakfast, Ace informed Peaches he was going home to get dressed and would return in a couple of hours. Getting into his black F-150, Ace pulled off down the street, arriving at his destination a few moments later. Walking into the house, he greeted Tori as she sat on the couch watching TV.

"Damn, I thought you wasn't ever gon' come see me. Like what the fuck, Ace? It's been two weeks. I know I'm not officially yo bitch yet but damn. Not seeing you ain't what the fuck I signed up for." Tori sat up from the couch, folding her arms and looking Ace directly in the eyes.

"I know, baby. And I apologize. A nigga just been real busy. You know Reason needs my help on top of what I already had going on. I just ain't had the time. But I'm here now. You gon' waste the time we do have arguing with me about not spending time, or you gon' love on me?" Ace asked, looking down at Tori. The gray two-piece outfit she wore curved to her body just right. "You lookin' thick as hell too. A nigga ain't tryin' to argue. I'm trying to do something else."

Tori licked her lips, not being able to keep her attitude with Ace. She walked over to him, wrapping her arms around his neck and pulling him down to her. "You tryin' to get that dick wet?" she whispered into his ear.

"Hell yeah, that's what a nigga need."

Ace unzipped his pants and walked over to the couch, taking a seat. He pulled out his rock-hard manhood and watched as Tori dropped to her knees in front of him, taking him into her mouth. She slurped and sucked, allowing her saliva to wet his rod as she opened her mouth wider. Positioning herself lower, she took both of his balls into her mouth, juggling them with her tongue. She simultaneously stroked his dick with her hand, sending Ace into an uproar.

"Damn, baby, that shit feel good as hell. You like sucking this dick?" Ace asked as his eyes rolled into the back of his head. Tori was the best at giving head, knowing every trick of the trade.

Not wanting Ace to cum before she was able to get hers, Tori stopped sucking and stood to her feet. She pulled her yoga pants down, and her round backside jiggled as she stepped out of them. Tori had gotten her body done two years ago and had been in the gym ever since, making sure to keep her body flawless. With her looks being her money-maker as a dancer at the most famous strip club in Detroit, she had to ensure her body always looked good.

"Oh, you want some of this dick, huh?" Ace whispered, removing a condom from his pocket and placing it onto his dick. "Bend that ass over and take this dick," Ace ordered. Grabbing her hips, he eased inside of her, biting his bottom lip at how good she felt. Tori's pussy was so good, Ace felt as though he was going to cum with each stroke. She was so wet and gushy that he heard every time he pumped in or out of her.

"Yeah, that pussy talking to me, huh? She sayin' she want this dick? Is that what she tellin' me?"

"Yes, Daddy, she telling you to pound her harder," Tori screamed.

Ace obliged, stroking both faster and harder. As much as he tried to hold off, he couldn't. Tori's pussy was too good, even with the condom on. He felt the sensation, and he let her know he was about to cum. No sooner than the words left his lips was he cumming.

"Damn, baby, that shit good as fuck. You need to start charging muthafuckas for that shit. That's too good to be givin' away for free. I feel like I need to throw you a stack just off GP."

"Well, if that's how you feel, hand that shit over. I ain't never gon' turn down no money. Leave that shit on the table on yo way out, nigga," she joked.

Ace, still serious, reached into his pocket and pulled out a wad of money before placing it onto her coffee table. "I gotta get outta here, but I'ma be back tomorrow."

"Yeah, that's the last thing you said before I saw you two weeks ago," Tori spoke, folding her arms.

"I'm for real, my baby. After what you just gave me, I'ma be back for real."

Ace kissed Tori on her forehead before walking out the door. He had one more stop to make before he headed home to get dressed. A few minutes later, he was pulling into Reason's driveway. Knocking on the door, he walked inside the home once Kalahni answered.

"What up doe? I just came to talk to Reason."

"He's in the living room. You can go in there, and I'll give you two some privacy."

Ace walked into the living room where Reason was sitting in his wheelchair. He was sitting in front of the TV, watching *John Wick*.

"What up doe, bro? How you feeling today?" Ace greeted.

"I'm good, just in here chillin'. What's up with you? What did you want to talk to me about?"

"Damn, you wanna get straight to it, huh? You don't wanna smoke a blunt first?" Ace laughed.

"Nah, I ain't smoking no more until I can walk again. I don't need nothing clouding my mind."

"I feel you on that. I already know yo ass ready to get out that wheelchair, and it's coming. You go to physical therapy tomorrow, right?"

"Yeah, and I can't wait. I really feel like this is going to be the best thing for me," Reason informed.

"And that's dope. I can't wait til you're back walkin' again."

"Yeah, me either, but enough with all that. What's up?"

"Well, I don't know if you know, but I want this to stay between us either way." Ace waited for Reason to agree before he spoke again. "Peaches been wanting to get out the game for a minute. She wanted to hand over the company to you. She was going to plan you a big ass party and hand over the organization. That was until your accident. Now, she feels like she needs to hold on to it until you heal. She been picking up the money from the spots and everything."

Reason looked at Ace, confused. "No, I didn't know that, but this is her organization. She been running this shit for years. So, I'm not sure what you trying to say, bro."

"She getting older though. And these niggas that's in the streets now ain't the same ones she dealt with back in the day. I don't want nothing happening to her. So, what if I took over until you healed? I mean, I'm already your right-hand," Ace suggested.

"Peaches good out here in these streets. She got respect on her name. Even these young niggas know what's up with her. They know what would go down if anything happened to her. If she want to get out the business, that's cool and all. But who runs it after that is not my decision to make. You need to talk to her about that."

Ace nodded his head, knowing he wasn't going to push the conversation any further. Ace knew Reason was far from dumb and didn't want him to suspect anything.

"Yeah, I know. I just thought it would be better if it came from you. But you're right. This is her organization, and she can hand it down to whomever she wants. I was just trying to help out. That's all."

Reason nodded his head, feeling that Ace's intentions were genuine. They sat there for several moments until Ace decided it was time for him to leave. He didn't have long before he had to be back to Peaches' house, and he still needed to change clothes. Saying his goodbyes to Reason, he walked out the door and got into his truck, pulling off down the street and heading home.

<hr>

After getting dressed, Ace made his way back to Peaches' house. After he rang her doorbell, Peaches answered wearing a cream one piece. Ace smiled as he looked at her. The fact that Peaches was in her late forties was something you wouldn't even know if she didn't tell you. Her body looked just like a woman in her twenties because her doctor had sculpted it perfectly. Her short pixie cut, that had been her signature style for years, was styled to perfection, and her makeup was flawless. She looked beautiful, and Ace couldn't help but smile.

"You ready to go, baby?" Ace asked, taking Peaches' hand into his.

Peaches looked at Ace and nodded her head. She was ready for the day Ace planned for them and couldn't wait to see what he had in store. They walked out the house, getting into Ace's truck before pulling off. As much as she liked Ace, she only hoped no one would see them out together. Reason was already going through a lot, and she didn't want to add to his stress.

Peaches was so deep in thought that she didn't realize there were at their destination until they pulled up. She looked around, not knowing where she was, as she looked at the all-white building.

"Where are we?" she asked.

"Come on, you will see."

Ace got out the car before walking around to the passenger's side and opening the door, holding his hand out. Peaches grabbed it before stepping down out the truck. They walked together hand in hand as they walked into the building. Peaches' mouth dropped open the moment they walked inside.

"Ace, what is this?" she asked, looking around.

"You love art, right? Well, I had a few of the up-and-coming artists from the city bring some of their best pieces together for you to choose from. This is your very own art show, and you can pick from any of the pieces you want. It's all for you, baby." Ace smiled.

Peaches didn't know what to say. She was so excited that she didn't know where to start. Dozens of beautiful paintings hung on the walls. She walked over to one of the pictures. It was a black and white painting of a naked woman sitting at a piano. She admired the painting, thinking about how beautiful it would look hanging in her living room.

"Can I offer you some champagne?" a waitress dressed in black pants and a white button up shirt asked.

Peaches smiled, taking one of the glasses from the tray in her hand. She sipped from the glass, eyes still on the painting.

"Do you like this one?" Ace asked.

"I love it. It's something both freeing and mysterious about this painting. I would love to hear about what the artist was thinking when they were painting this masterpiece."

"Why don't you ask him yourself? He's right over there." Ace pointed out. He was conversing with two other men and a woman.

"I can't just go over there and interrupt them. They could be having an important conversation."

"I can ensure you they're not. They are all here for you. I put this entire event together for us to enjoy. Why do you think nobody is here but us? The artists are here to answer any questions that you might have. Go over there and ask him whatever questions you have for him."

Ace watched as Peaches walked over to the group of artists. He'd known this was something Peaches would enjoy. They stayed at the gallery for a few hours, and Ace purchased several paintings for her, setting them up to be delivered to her home the next day.

"Are you ready for the next part of our date?" Ace asked.

"What more can you possibly have planned? You have bought me every painting that I loved in the gallery," Peaches gushed.

"I told you I have an entire day planned for us, baby. Shit, this can last all night if you want it to. I don't have to be anywhere besides where you are."

Peaches smiled, ready to accompany Ace anywhere he would lead her. About twenty minutes later, they pulled up to a park. Peaches looked around, confused. She was not expecting a park to be the next thing on their agenda. Once again, Ace got out the truck and walked around to the passenger side, opening Peaches' door for her. He took her hand and guided her through the park. They walked for about five minutes before they stopped at a huge beige tent.

"Ace, what's this?" Peaches asked, perplexed.

"How 'bout we go inside, so you can see?" Ace suggested, unzipping the tent and leading Peaches inside. Her mouth dropped open when she saw what Ace had done for her. The tent was filled with white hanging lights and red roses. There was a table on the far side of the tent which housed chilled champagne and several plates that were covered with cloches. On the other side of the tent was a smaller candlelit table and two chairs along with a huge cream floor pillow and a blanket. The entire space was beautiful and beyond anything that Peaches was expecting.

"Ace, I don't even know what to say. This is amazing."

"You deserve all this and more. Why don't you have a seat, and I'll make your plate?"

Peaches obliged, taking her seat at the table. Ace placed her dinner plate in front of her. The stuffed lobster tail, jumbo lump crab cake, and asparagus looked delicious. Once Ace sat down opposite her, they both began eating.

"I hope you are enjoying this date. I wanted to put something very special together for you."

"And you did, Ace. This was the most thoughtful thing anyone has ever done for me. I can tell you put a lot of thought into this, and nobody has ever done anything like this for me before." Peaches smiled.

"You deserve all this and more. That's something I don't think you understand, baby. I want to give you everything. I want to make your most unthinkable dreams come true," Ace spoke, leaning over the table and kissing her softly on the lips. They spent several hours in the tent, talking about life and what the future held for them. Peaches, not wanting the night to end, asked Ace to spend the night at her house. Of course Ace accepted her invitation, knowing that she would be wrapped around his fingers in no time. They spent the rest of the night making love.

Chapter Five

Kalahni had just finished helping Reason get dressed for the day when the doorbell rang. Thinking it was Peaches, Kalahni rushed to the door and opened it. Much to her surprise, Tori and her nephew, Brayden, stood on the other side.

"Hey, girl. What's up?" Kalahni asked, stepping to the side, so Tori and Brayden could enter the house.

"Well, my sister asked me to watch Brayden today, and I decided to take him to Chuck E, Cheese. We stopped by to see if Easton could go with us. Brayden says he misses him."

"Aww, that's sweet, Tori. I'm sure Easton would love to go to Chuck E. Cheese with you. He just asked me about you the other day, Brayden. He's upstairs playing his game. I'll go get him."

Kalahni walked up the stairs and returned a few moments later with a smiling Easton. Tori informed her that she would bring him back later, and they walked out the door. Kalahni was happy that Tori had come to pick up Easton. With Reason about to go to his physical therapy session, she would have the house all to herself. She was in desperate need of some alone time and was going to take full advantage of the moment.

"Where did Tori say she was taking Easton?" Reason asked, taking his lift chair down the stairs. Kalahni helped him into his wheelchair before answering.

"Oh, he's gon' love that. We all know how much lil man loves Chuck E. Cheese. Damn, that means you're about to have the entire house to yourself. What you plan to do with that time?"

"Shit, I'm just gonna chill. Probably take a hot bubble bath, maybe give myself a facial. Who knows?"

"Yeah, that sounds good. Maybe me and my mom will go out to eat after my therapy session. That way you will have more alone time. I know this situation has been stressful for you, and I know a self-care day would help," Reason suggested. He wanted to do everything he could to show Kalahni that he really didn't want to be a burden on her or anyone else for that matter. He knew it had to be hard taking care of a grown man, and he felt if he gave her some space and some time to relax, she would feel a lot better.

Kalahni smiled and nodded her head in agreement. She was happy that Reason understood what she was going through. Several moments later, the doorbell chimed again. Kalahni went to answer it, certain it was Peaches. However, this time, she looked out the peephole just to confirm. Seeing it was indeed her, she opened the door and allowed her entry to their home.

"Hey, y'all. How is everything on this beautiful morning?" Peaches greeted cheerfully.

"Everything is great, Ma. I see you're in a good mood this morning." Reason smiled.

"I'm just excited about your next physical therapy appointment. This appointment brings you one step closer to walking again. This is a wonderful day." Peaches beamed.

"Yes, it is," Kalahni agreed with a smile.

"Where my grandson at? I want to see him before we leave."

"He's not here. My friend, Tori, just came and picked him up," Kalahni informed. She was sick of the small talk and ready for the two of them to leave.

"Oh, okay. Well, I guess I'll just have to see him later then. Are you ready to go, Reason?"

"Yeah, I'm ready when you are."

Kalahni followed them out to Peaches' car. She helped Peaches put Reason into the car before placing his wheelchair into her trunk. She waited for Peaches to pull off before going back into the house. Doing exactly what she said she was going to do, she headed upstairs to run herself a bubble bath. After walking into her bedroom, she headed downstairs to prepare herself a mimosa. When she was finished, she headed back up to her bedroom and grabbed her laptop from her nightstand.

Once back inside her bathroom, she placed both her laptop and glass onto her bath shelf. She opened the Netflix app on her laptop and went to the latest season of *The Circle*. She lit several scented candles around the bathroom before taking off her clothes and easing down into the hot, soapy water. She pressed play on her laptop and picked up her glass, taking a large sip. She smiled at the bubbly sweetness of the cranberry mimosa as it eased down her throat.

Kalahni was about fifteen minutes into her bubble bath when she heard her doorbell chime. At first, she wasn't going to answer it, then she thought it might be Tori bringing Easton home early. Pushing her bath shelf down her claw foot tub, she stood to her feet and got out the water, quickly drying herself with a towel before sliding into her red Versace robe. Heading down the steps, Kalahni looked out the peephole before opening the door.

"Damn, did I catch you at shower time?" Ace asked, walking through the door.

"Something like that. I was taking a bubble bath. What's up?" Kalahni asked.

"What you mean what's up? You already know why I'm here," Ace announced, grabbing Kalahni and pulling her to him. He kissed her lips passionately, savoring the taste of them. "I missed you, and I know he went to physical therapy today. You should have already knew I was gon' be comin' through."

"I missed you too, baby. I don't know how much longer I can pretend not to have feelings for you," Kalahni replied.

"It's not gon' be too much longer, baby. I promise. I got a plan, and I know this shit gon' work. You just gotta hold on a little while longer. Then, the world will be ours. We gon' be good, baby," Ace assured.

Kalahni smiled and kissed Ace once more. She believed in him and his plan, knowing it would set them up real nice. She knew Ace loved her, so there was no need to question him. She was just tired of hiding it and ready to make their love public. She began fucking Ace over three years ago and had been in love with him ever since. Before the accident, she couldn't bear to tell Reason the truth. He had all the money, and she knew she was nothing without him. However, helping him with all his needs after an accident was never in her plan. She didn't know how temporary his condition would be, but she knew if the money ever ran out, she was gone.

"Where is my son?" Ace asked, stepping into the living room and taking a seat on the couch.

"My homegirl, Tori, came to pick him up for a playdate with her nephew. So, we got the house to ourselves," Kalahni answered.

When Kalahni and Ace first started fucking, they never knew they would fall so deep in love. However, when Kalahni did fall in love with Ace, she was so into Reason's money that she couldn't allow Ace to be her main nigga. Ace agreed with that at the time because his feelings were not as strong for Kalahni as hers were for him. On top of that, Reason was his best friend. They were like brothers, and he couldn't bear to expose the fact that he'd been fucking his girl right under his nose. However, when Kalahni got pregnant with Easton, it was a different story. He was well aware there would be a question of paternity the moment Kalahni informed him of her pregnancy; a DNA test was a must. With Kalahni not wanting to tell Reason the truth until she absolutely had to, they both thought it best if Ace was the first person tested.

When the DNA test came back with Ace being Easton's father, Ace was ready to be the family man he knew Kalahni and his son needed. However, Kalahni was scared to lose the money that Reason came with. Knowing that if she stayed with him, she and her son would have the best life possible, Kalahni was able to talk Ace into allowing Reason to think he was the father, assuring Ace that one day they would tell the truth and be together.

After that, Ace formed a plan. He needed to get as much money as he could in order to get his family back. He was sick of Reason being the one to have everything. Even when they were kids, he had all the latest everything while Ace, on the other hand, grew up poor with nothing. It wasn't until Peaches finally put his mother on the payroll that they finally started seeing some real money. Ace felt like no matter how hard he tried, he was always in Reason's shadow. Reason had everything, including his family, and he knew he would have to do something. So, he came up with a plan to take the very organization that made him who he was while making him the top supplier in the state of Michigan.

"Oh, so ain't nobody here, huh? I been waiting for this." Ace licked his lips.

"Oh, you been waiting on it, huh? Then show me how much you missed it," Kalahni challenged, untying her robe and exposing her naked body underneath. Ace smiled at her thickness, quickly unzipping his pants and pulling her on top of him. They both moaned upon entry — Kalahni at his rock-hard manhood that she'd been missing and Ace at her tight wetness.

"Baby, I love you so much!" Kalahni called out as she rode his dick like a horse. His manhood felt big and strong inside of her.

"I love you too, baby. This shit feels so good. This my pussy, baby? Tell me this pussy is mine!" Ace called out as he pumped harder.

"Yesssss, Daddy, this pussy is yours!"

Kalahni bounced up and down as Ace clutched her hips. They both felt their climax nearing, and their moans became louder. Kalahni wrapped her hands around Ace's neck before kissing him passionately. They both reached their orgasm at the same time. They laid on the couch in each other's arms for several moments before finally breaking their embrace.

"How long we got before he comes back?" Ace asked.

"Shit, probably about an hour or so, maybe a little longer if he goes out to eat with Peaches, but I'm not sure."

"It's all good. Maybe I will just head out and come back later. How about we plan a date so that we can spend some real time together? It's been a minute, and I don't like how you got to spend all yo time taking care of Reason."

"Yeah, me either. I actually hate that shit. I'm ready for us to be a real family. I'm sick of living this lie. And the quicker we stop, the quicker I can be happy again."

"It's coming, baby. I promise. I got a game plan that's in motion that I promise you will set us up for life. We bout to be on top of the world. I just gotta handle some shit first."

"I got you, babe. I'ma be waiting on you."

Kalahni kissed Ace once more before standing up from the couch. Ace fixed his clothes before hugging Kalahni and walking out the door. Kalahni made her way back upstairs and into the bathroom. She ran herself another bubble bath and stepped down into the tub, watching an episode of her favorite show as she soaked.

"I know it might be a little too early to say this, but I feel like you will be walking before we know it. The fact that this is only our second therapy session and you are already starting to move your toes is wonderful. I've never seen anyone move so fast in all the years I've been doing this." Serenity smiled.

They had all just witnessed Reason wiggling his toes, and it was such a proud moment for everyone involved. Reason was the happiest though, smiling from ear to ear. This was the biggest ego boost Reason had in a long time. He knew that Serenity would be the key to his healing, and he was happy that she was chosen to be his physical therapist.

"See, son, you're going to be walking in no time. We definitely about to go out to eat after this. We got something to celebrate now!" Peaches cheered.

Reason was proud of himself. Although he knew he still had a long way to go, this was definitely a step in the right direction. The first thing he thought about was telling Kalahni. He couldn't wait to see the smile on her face. To finally see some light at the end of a dark tunnel was exactly what they all needed.

"Serenity, thank you. I know I owe this all to you and the work you speak so highly of."

"There is no need to thank me, Reason. I enjoy doing all this, and I'm happy this is working so quickly for you." Serenity smiled.

"You really are wonderful at what you do. Your hands and mind are truly blessed," Reason complimented.

"Thank you, but I'm not the one that gets the credit for any of this. It's your hard work and dedication that is paying off."

"Either way, I am thankful. My son is getting better, and I'm not sure it would have happened so quickly if it wasn't for you." Peaches beamed.

This was the best Reason had felt in months. His ego was boosted, and he was ready to take on the world. Thanking Serenity one more time, Reason wheeled himself out of the room and out to Peaches' car with one male nurse coming to help him get inside. Him and Peaches went out to lunch, ready to celebrate the win the family had just gotten. Today had turned out to be a great day, and Reason couldn't wait to have an even better night.

***

Tori dropped Easton off around six that evening before heading home herself. She hoped Ace was coming to see her. She missed him and wanted to feel him inside her. She was tired of being placed on the back burner. She needed Ace to see her for what she was, and that was his ride or die. Tori was well aware of Ace's dream of being the biggest drug kingpin Detroit had ever seen. So, she vowed to do anything in her power to help him get there with her dream being to be the wife of the biggest drug kingpin. She thought that if she helped Ace accomplish his dreams, he would help her accomplish hers.

Walking into the kitchen, Tori grabbed a spiked Simply Lemonade before pouring it into a glass. She needed to put together a plan so that Ace would be in position to take over. Walking over to her purse, she took her iPhone out and shot a text to her cousin, asking him if he would stop by for a minute. He texted her back a few seconds later, letting her know he was already in the area and would be there in about five minutes.

When there was a knock at her door exactly five minutes later, she knew it was her cousin. Opening the door for him and allowing him in, she turned the deadbolt lock on the door just in case Ace chose to come by while her cousin was there. Ace had a key, but if the deadbolt was on, there would be no way he could get in unless Tori opened it.

"What up doe, Kilo? Thank you for stopping by. I got some shit I want to talk to you about."

"What up doe, cuz? What you got going on?" Kilo asked, taking a seat at Tori's kitchen table. He pulled out a bag of weed and a Backwood from his pants pocket. He knew if his cousin called him to come over, he was definitely going to need a blunt to get him through the reason why.

"I need some shit handled, and this time, I need it handled for real. We can't have another situation like last time. I need this shit to be fool proof and carried out right," Tori explained.

"What you mean not like last time? I came through for you last time. You wanted that nigga, Reason, out, and he out. I heard that nigga was paralyzed. Last time I checked, ain't nobody in the hood scared of a paralyzed ass nigga," Kilo responded.

"Yeah, but that nigga is still alive. He still fucking breathing, and that keeps him in the way. I told you to shoot that nigga, not hit him with your car. And let's keep this shit a bean. He the one that called the hit that got Brick killed."

"Yeah, let's keep that shit a bean for real. And the truth is, niggas in the hood say Ace called that hit. So, if I gotta put down anybody behind Brick, it's that nigga."

Tori's eyes widened at the mention of Ace's name. She didn't want Ace getting hurt because he was the reason she was doing this. He was her ticket out, so she needed to make sure he had everything he needed to come up. Him being hurt in the process was not in the cards, so Tori would make sure that Ace's name stayed far away from this plan.

"Ace might be the one that relayed the message, but that shit came from Reason. You hit a lick on Reason's spots, and then he got into that accident. With Ace being his right-hand man, he was only doing what he was told to do. You can't fault him for doing his job. I'm telling you, Reason is the one you want. If he dead, the hit on you would be over."

Kilo nodded his head, feeling like his cousin could be right. He just needed to hear more about her plan before he fully agreed. He didn't know how she expected him to get to Reason. With him being paralyzed, he wasn't pulling up to the hood. *Shit, me pulling up to his house and taking him out would be a death sentence. I know he got all kinds of security with him being paralyzed and all,* Kilo assumed. He sat there, listening to everything Tori said, taking in each word.

As much as he wanted to kill the person responsible for his brother's death, he didn't feel that Reason was the person responsible. His first mind was telling him that Ace was just as much to blame as Reason was — if not more. He would allow his cousin to think whatever she wanted to, but he knew who needed to feel his revenge. He didn't understand why she was trying to save Ace anyway. In Kilo's eyes, both of them needed to be dead, and that was something he was more than ready to do. He left Tori's house that night with nothing but murder on his mind as he headed back to his safe house.

Chapter Six

Two weeks had passed, and Reason was showing a vast improvement. Although he was still in his wheelchair, he was able to move his feet. The feeling was starting to come back in his legs, and he knew it wouldn't be long before he was up and walking again. He sat on the floor with Serenity in front of him. Their session had just started, and she was giving him a massage, the same thing she did at the beginning of every session. She poured the heated oil into her hands and rubbed it all over Reason's legs and feet. Serenity smiled as she looked over at him.

"Why you looking at me like that?" Reason asked, laughing nervously.

"I just want to know your story. Who is Reason Alexander? I know you are a son with a mother that will go to the ends of the earth for you. But that's all I know."

"What else you wanna know? I'll tell you anything," Reason assured.

"I wanna know everything about you. Like are you a father? What do you do for a living?"

"I'm in real estate," Reason lied. "And I have a two-year-old son named Easton. He's my pride and joy. I swear he's the reason I'm working so hard to get better. I gotta be here for him. What about you? Do you have any kids?"

Serenity continued to rub as she nodded her head. "I do. I have a little girl. She's three, and her name is Scotland. That's my little diva." Serenity continued his massage before starting Reason's leg exercises.

Reason watched how delicately she handled him, moving his limbs with care. He'd known she was beautiful from the first time he met her, but today she took his breath away. She was the most beautiful woman that he'd ever seen. Her caramel skin was flawless, even without makeup, and Reason wanted to touch it to see if it was as soft as it looked. *Come on, nigga, you can't be on yo old bullshit. As pretty as she is, she is your PT. Get yo shit together, Reason.*

"So, what's your story? What made you get into physical therapy?"

Reason saw Serenity's eyes fill with water, and he instantly wished he could take back the question. "If it's going to open old wounds, you don't have to answer. I was just trying to make small talk," Reason spoke. He saw her reaction and knew there was pain behind her story. He didn't want to bring up any past trauma that might cause Serenity sadness and thought it best to just change the subject altogether, but before he could, Serenity spoke.

"No, it's fine. When I was thirteen, my grandmother was in a horrible car accident which paralyzed her. Something like yourself. She got into such a deep depression and just couldn't get out of it. She went to different physical therapists, and they all gave up on her. I just felt if she had at least one in her corner, it could have changed her life. They all gave up on her, which ultimately made her give up on herself. I was too young to help her then. So, after that, I vowed to help everyone that I could. I became a physical therapist to ensure that none of my patients' families felt the way I did."

Reason saw her tears fall, and he lifted his hand to wipe them away. It was so instinctive that he didn't even realize he'd done it. Serenity placed her hand on his, holding it there for a couple of seconds. Reason looked into her eyes, and in that moment, he saw a beautiful woman with a lot of pain behind her. He didn't see the physical therapist that helped everyone else heal. He saw the woman that had healed herself, and she was beautiful. He opened his mouth to speak, but Serenity's words came first.

"Let's put these weights on your legs, so we can move on to the next exercise."

Reason nodded his head, letting go of the conversation and allowing Serenity to place the weights on his legs. They did a few rounds of leg workouts before Serenity removed the weights. Before Reason knew it, their hour-long session was over. However, Reason wasn't ready to leave. He wanted to stay in her presence a while longer; however, he knew their session was over. *Let me get the fuck up outta here and stop lookin' thirsty. You got a whole family at home, my nigga. What the fuck is wrong with you?*

Shane walked into the room a few moments later to help Reason into his wheelchair. He thanked him before letting Serenity know he would see her at his next session. He wheeled himself out to the waiting room where Peaches was sitting

When Reason got home, he found that neither Kalahni or Easton were there. Peaches helped him in the house and asked if he wanted her to stay with him. When he declined, Peaches nodded her head and walked out the house. With Reason being home alone, he was going to use this time to handle some business. Grabbing his phone, he placed a call to Ace. He wanted to figure out what was going on with Kilo. It had been weeks, and he still hadn't gotten word that he'd been taken care of.

He called Ace twice, and he didn't answer either time. Reason decided that he would wait and try calling Ace back later. He spent the rest of the day sitting in the living room, watching TV, waiting on Easton and Kalahni to return home.

***

Kalahni jumped out of Ace's bed once she looked over at the clock. It was close to three in the morning, and she knew she needed to get home. She'd fallen asleep without setting her alarm, and she couldn't believe Ace had let her sleep so long. Rushing into the bathroom, she took a quick shower, not wanting to go home smelling like sex. Once she was dressed, she woke Ace to let him know she was leaving.

"I don't know why you rushing back home. It's already three in the morning. You might as well just stay here for the night."

"Shit, you already know I want to. You was the one that said we had to keep playing this role. I don't even want to go back there. The nigga is useless. I wanna stay right here with you and that dick," Kalahni announced, grabbing a handful of Ace's manhood.

"Okay, nah, don't start nothing you can't finish, my baby."

"I might not can finish it tonight, but when Reason takes his crippled ass to his therapy session on Friday, you can definitely come over."

Ace nodded his head, letting Kalahni know he would do just that. He kissed her softly on her lips before walking her to the door. He watched her walk to the car and pull out his driveway before closing his door. He walked back into the bedroom and rolled himself a blunt before sitting on his bed. He took several pulls from the blunt before his cell phone started ringing.

"Who the fuck is calling me at this time of night? This shit better be about some money." Ace grabbed his phone and saw that it was Reason. With this being the third time he'd called, Ace decided to answer.

"What up doe, my nigga?" Ace greeted.

"Dawg, I think something is wrong. Kalahni and Easton were gone when I got home and here it is, three in the morning, and she still ain't here. I've been calling her nonstop, and she ain't even answering. I swear if that nigga, Kilo, did anything to them, I'm gonna kill that nigga with my bare fucking hands. This is why that Kilo shit should have been handled."

"Reason, calm down, bro. What makes you think something happened to her? And why would Kilo get at Kalahni and Easton? That nigga know the code of the streets, so he knows women and children are off limits. I just can't see him doing shit to either of them."

"That nigga didn't know the code of the streets when he was robbing my spots. And you expect me to believe he magically started livin' by street code now? Come on, my baby. You gotta be smarter than that."

"Okay, chill on me, my nigga. You over here in yo feelings about a bitch that probably just went out with her homegirls. She probably on her way home right now, and you over here accusing a nigga of hurting her and Easton? I don't get it. You tryin' to start a war that you can't fight?" Ace was clearly irritated and was ready to end the call.

Man, I know that bitch pussy good and all, but I damn sure ain't bout to be looking around in the daytime with a flashlight for no bitch. This nigga can't even walk, but he wanna chase a bitch? Shit don't even make sense, Ace thought to himself as he shook his head.

"Nigga, don't think that just because I'm in this wheelchair that I can't buss a pistol. My legs might not work, but my hands work just fine. Ace, you're supposed to be my right-hand. You want me to talk my mama into handing over the company to you, but you can't even follow simple instructions. I told you to..."

Kalahni walked in the house, stopping Reason midsentence. Looking up at Kalahni, he told Ace he would call him back and ended the call. He looked Kalahni up and down and didn't see a hair out of place. She had also walked in the door alone. As happy as he was that she was safe, he wanted to know where she'd been and why Easton wasn't with her.

"Where the fuck have you been, and where is my son? It's after three in the morning, and I've been calling and calling you."

"My bad, baby. I was out with Tori downtown at the casino. You know we can't have no phones out while you on the table, so I just left mine in the car when we went in. I didn't even look at my phone when I got in the car. It was so late when we got outta there, my ass just came straight home," Kalahni lied.

Reason just looked at her, trying to detect any signs that she wasn't being truthful. When he couldn't find any, he went on to his next question. "Where is Easton?"

"He's at my mom's house. I'ma go pick him up in the morning. We can just chill together for the rest of the night. We needed some time alone anyway," Kalahni suggested.

"The night is over. You should have been home hours ago if you wanted to spend some fuckin' time with me. I'm going to bed."

Reason wheeled himself to his lift chair and headed upstairs. He knew Kalahni was lying to him about where she'd been; he just couldn't prove it. He wanted to know where she was but knew there was no way she was going to tell him the truth. So, instead of arguing, he wheeled himself to the bed and went to sleep.

The next afternoon, Reason woke up to the smell of breakfast being made. Before he could even get out the bed, Kalahni walked into the room to wake him up.

"Good morning, baby. I made you brunch. You want me to help get you dressed before you go downstairs?"

"Yeah, that's cool. Thanks, babe. What time you going to get Easton? I don't want him over there too long. Plus I want to spend some time with him today." Reason didn't even speak on the events that took place the night before, knowing it would only start an argument. He knew that what was done in the dark would eventually come to the light, so he chose to sit back and allow things to reveal itself.

"I'll go get him after we eat. Do you want to go with me?"

Reason nodded his head, and Kalahni wheeled him to the bathroom and ran the shower. She helped him into the shower chair and began washing his body. When she was done, she dried him off and helped him back into his wheelchair before going back into their room and getting him dressed.

After brunch, they both made their way over to Kalahni's mother's house to pick up Easton. It was a nice day outside for it to be early November in Detroit. The sun was shining, and the temperature was in the low seventies, which was unusual for that time of year. When they pulled up to Kalahni's mother's house, she asked Reason to stay in the car while she went in to get Easton. She knew Reason didn't really care for her mother, and it was because of the way her mother treated her. Reason saw Michelle as a horrible mother. She treated Kalahni as her own personal ATM, and when Kalahni didn't give Michelle money, she would curse her out and talk down to her to the point where Kalahni would be in tears. Reason remembered one incident in particular when Michelle wanted to take a trip to Cancun. She'd basically made all the plans at Kalahni's expense, which was really Reason's expense. When Kalahni told her she wouldn't be able to get the money, Michelle was furious. She placed a call to CPS, making a claim that Kalahni was abusing Easton. Although Reason couldn't prove that it was her, he knew no one else could be so cruel.

Kalahni was only in the house for a few minutes before coming back out with Easton. Reason smiled, greeting his son. Easton was happy to see him as well, wrapping his tiny arms around Reason's neck, hugging him.

"I missed you, Daddy. Can we watch *Spider-Man* when we get home? Grandma didn't have it on her TV."

"Of course we can. But first, how about we go to the park? It's a nice, sunny day outside, and the fresh air would do us all some good." Reason looked over to Kalahni for a response.

Before she could speak, Easton chimed in. "Yeah, let's go to the park. I wanna play on the slide and the swings."

"Well, I guess we going to the park then," Kalahni agreed, starting the car and pulling off down the street on their way to the park.

<hr>

Tori lay naked on Ace's chest as she twisted his beard through her fingers. Rolling over, Tori grabbed the blunt that was sitting in the ashtray on her nightstand. She lit it, taking a few pulls before passing it to Ace. "If I asked you a question, would you tell me the truth?"

"It depends on what it is. But tell me what's on yo mind, Tori."

"Word around the hood is you put a hit on Kilo's head. Is that true?" Tori asked. She had been keeping the fact that Kilo was her cousin from Ace. However, she now thought it might work out better for her if she told him.

"It's a hit on him, but I ain't the one who put it out. Why you askin' about that shit?" Ace passed the blunt back to Tori.

"What if I told you I could help you get DP's organization faster?"

"In real life, my baby, if you could do that shit, we would both be straight. I would take care of you, and you would have everything you could ever ask for, but the real question is how. How could you get me her organization?"

"Do you trust me?" Tori asked, taking another pull. She exhaled a cloud of smoke before speaking again. "I mean, like really trust me?"

"What you getting at, my baby? Tell me what's up. You know I trust you if I sleep with you at night. So, just tell me what's up," Ace answered.

"If Reason was gone, then you would be next in line to run the company, correct?"

"I mean, I guess, but that would only be if Peaches stepped down. But what you mean if Reason was gone? How would that even happen?"

Tori looked into Ace's eyes and took a deep breath. She didn't know how he would react to what she was about to say. Knowing there was no need to sugarcoat anything, she just came out and said it. "Kilo is my cousin."

Ace's eyes widened as he jumped out of bed. He picked his pants up from the floor and grabbed his pistol before Tori even knew what was happening. "Fuck is this shit, some kind of setup? Fuck you mean that nigga is yo cousin?" Ace yelled, aiming his gun directly at Tori.

"Baby, calm down. It ain't even like that. I'm trying to show you that we can all work together. The three of us together will get you to the spot you need, baby. I'm just tryin' to show you I'm yo ride or die."

Ace couldn't believe what he was hearing. As much as he hoped that it was the weed that had him tripping, he knew that he was hearing everything Tori was saying loud and clear.

"I'm only trying to help, and I know my plan would work. I would never try to set you up, baby. You gotta believe me," Tori pleaded, holding both hands up in surrender.

"If Kilo yo cousin, that means Brick is too. You want me to believe you don't want revenge for that? You could be setting up both me and Reason for all I fuckin' know."

Tori shook her head. Although she didn't think Ace would shoot her, she continued to hold her hands in the air. "If that was the case, then why would I tell you? Do you know how many nights you slept right here in my bed next to me? If I wanted you dead, I had more than a few chances to make that happen. Yet you standing here still breathing, holding a fuckin' gun on me. Think about it, Ace."

Ace began to lower his gun. He knew that what Tori was saying was making sense. If she wanted him dead, he would have been. *Damn, maybe this bitch is tellin' the truth. I might as well hear her out,* Ace thought, taking a seat back on Tori's bed.

"Tell me your plan, Tori."

Reason made his way to his therapy session, eager to see Serenity. She'd been on his mind heavy since the last time he saw her. His last conversation with Serenity lifted layers of her he didn't even know was there. He wanted to know more about the amazing woman that was healing him. Until that day, his mother was the strongest woman Reason knew. However now, Reason felt Serenity and Peaches were running neck and neck. Serenity healed herself from her own trauma while still being able to heal others from theirs. That was something that Reason admired.

Wheeling himself back into the room, he waited patiently until Serenity walked inside, her smile brightening the entire room when she walked in the door. "Good afternoon, Reason. How are you doing today?"

"I'm great now that I'm here." Reason smiled back. "How are you doing?"

"I'm good, but I do have something I want to talk to you about," Serenity announced, taking a seat in the chair next to Reason.

"What's up, Serenity?"

"Well, I'm not sure how my office is just catching this, but we never got your insurance information. My secretary was under the impression the hospital had faxed all the information over to us while I just thought she'd gotten your information from you during your first visit. I have no problem billing your insurance company for all of our past sessions; we just need your insurance card to do so. Do you happen to have it on you?"

"No, I don't. It's at home. But I can have my mama run back to the house and get it," Reason assured.

"Nah, you don't have to do all that. You can just bring it when you come for your next session."

"Hell no, you been waiting on yo money long enough. Let me call her." Reason pulled his phone from his pocket. He placed a call to Peaches, who was sitting out in the waiting room, asking her to go back to his house to get his insurance card before letting her know exactly where it was. Without a second thought, Peaches made her way to her car, heading back to Reason's house.

Chapter Seven

"I can't stay long, baby. I got so much to do. But I wanted to stop by because I missed you and told you I would come," Ace explained as soon as Kalahni let him in the house.

"It's all good, baby. I'm just happy you came. I missed you too, and I'm happy to see you."

"Where is Easton?" Ace asked.

"I just put him down for a nap. We won't have any distractions."

Ace nodded his head, and Kalahni led him to the couch. She had on nothing but a silk robe, and when she took it off, she revealed her perfect body. Ace walked over to her, taking one of her double D breasts into his mouth and sucking on it. Kalahni moaned, tossing her head back in pleasure. Ace allowed his other hand to travel downward, resting between Kalahni's legs. She moaned a bit louder when he slid two of his fingers inside her.

"Lay down, baby. Let Daddy taste that pussy," Ace whispered.

Kalahni did as she was told, lying flat on the couch and spreading her thighs for Ace. Getting on his knees, he positioned himself in front of Kalahni, twirling her nipples in his fingers as his soft tongue savored her precious jewel. Kalahni wrapped her legs around Ace's shoulders as she moaned softly. He was eating her pussy like he was on death row, and this was his last meal. His tongue told a story of a man that had been longing to taste her as he savored her juices.

Ace ate her until he felt her body become limp. Her legs dropped to the floor, and her breaths were heavy. Unzipping his jeans, he pulled out his manhood before easing it into Kalahni's wetness, both moaning upon entry. He pumped in and out of her slowly as she held him tightly.

"It feels so good, baby," Kalahni whispered into Ace's ear.

"This yo dick, baby. Get on top so you can ride it."

With those words, they switched positions, placing Kalahni on top. She grinded on him slowly, keeping the same rhythm. Ace bit his bottom lip as he cupped both of her breasts in his hands, his toes curling as his climax neared.

"Damn, baby, I can't hold this shit. This pussy 'bout to make a nigga cum," Ace called out.

Kalahni took that as her sign, and she clenched her walls around his manhood tightly as she began to thrust harder. Ace placed his hands on her hips as he guided her movements. Before he knew it, he was cumming and so was she. Breathing hard, Kalahni laid on Ace's chest, his manhood still resting inside her.

"That shit felt so good, baby. You better stop before I end up putting another baby inside you," Ace spoke, wrapping his arms tightly around Kalahni's naked body.

"Would that be a bad thing? I'm ready for us to be a real family now more than ever. It's time for Easton to know who his real daddy is."

After Reason's accident, Kalahni knew the money he had wouldn't last long. She knew Peaches would make sure Reason was good, but the money she was accustomed to spending on the daily would be gone. Knowing that Ace was on his way to the top, she felt it was only right for her to take her rightful seat on the throne next to Ace as his queen.

"It's coming, baby. I promise. I just want to make sure I'm in a position to take care of us as well as protect us. They gonna be mad when they find this out, and it's more than likely gon' cause a lot of problems. I need to ensure I can handle everything that comes our way. Just give me a little more time, baby. I promise it won't be much longer."

Kalahni nodded her head, knowing that what Ace was saying made sense. She knew when their secret came out, it wouldn't only be Reason that was upset. Peaches loved Easton with all her heart, and this would truly crush her. With Kalahni already knowing how Peaches felt about her, she knew this would be the icing on the cake. This would be Peaches' reason to kill her, and Kalahni knew it. So, with that, she agreed with Ace, keeping their love a secret for a few moments longer.

"I gotta get outta here, my baby. I got a lot of shit I gotta do. I'ma hit you up tomorrow if you can get away."

Kalahni agreed, kissing him once more before climbing off of him. Ace put his clothes back on before hugging Kalahni and walking out the door. Kalahni was just about to walk upstairs to take a shower when there was a knock at the door. *What this nigga forget?* Kalahni thought to herself as she walked over to the door. She swung it open, already knowing it was Ace.

"What you le... Peaches?" Kalahni yelled out her name two octaves louder than she meant to. Saying she was stunned was an understatement. *What the fuck is she doing here? She's supposed to be at Reason's physical therapy session with him. Lord, did she see Ace just leave? She had to. There was no way she didn't. He literally just walked out the door.* Kalahni's hands began to sweat as she became nervous.

"Were you expecting someone else?" Peaches asked, looking Kalahni up and down suspiciously. Peaches walked into the house, and she instantly smelled the sex in the air. She saw Ace when he pulled out of Reason's driveway, and the moment Kalahni came to the door in her robe, Peaches knew what it was.

"I thought you were Tori; she just left. She needed to borrow one of my purses," Kalahni lied. She figured if Peaches only saw a car, she wouldn't really know who was inside. She knew it was a long shot, but she had to try something. When Peaches just nodded her head, Kalahni knew she hadn't seen anything.

"I had to come back here to get Reason's insurance card. He already told me where it was, so I'm just gonna run up and get it." Without another word, Peaches made her way up the stairs and into Reason's room. She was furious and was ready to beat the shit out of Kalahni. *This bitch must think I'm some kind of a fuckin' fool. Tori my mutha-fuckin' ass. I would recognize Ace anywhere. I been getting that dick. Now he fuckin' on Kalahni too? Fuck is this nigga on?*

Peaches didn't know what to do as she paced back-and-forth. "Man, this shit is gon' crush Reason. How this nigga, Ace, fucking his mama and his bitch?" Peaches asked herself. She was ready to blow every fucking thing to the ground. She didn't know what she wanted to do first. *Do I tell Reason what's going on, or do I confront Ace first?* Grabbing Reason's insurance card, she walked out of his room, still not knowing what her next move would be.

Peaches was in deep thought her entire ride back to Reason. She had to admit her feelings were hurt. She would have never thought that Ace would do anything like this to her. Peaches thought that Ace really loved her. To find out now that everything had been a lie was heartbreaking.

"I just don't understand what Ace would get out of doing this shit. I need to figure out what the fuck is going on before I involve Reason," Peaches spoke out loud to herself as she pulled into the parking lot. Pulling her visor down, she looked into the mirror. She needed to ensure Reason wouldn't be able to look at her and tell anything was wrong. Walking back into the office, Peaches handed Reason's insurance card to the receptionist.

About twenty minutes later, Reason was wheeling himself out into the waiting room. Once out to the car, one of the male nurses helped him inside.

"You ready to go home, or you want to come back to my house for a minute?" Peaches asked, looking over to Reason.

"Nah, I wanna go home. I wanna do some more leg exercises. I'm starting to get the feeling back in my legs, and Serenity says if I'm able to stay up at our next session, then I will be able to practice walking." Reason beamed.

Peaches looked over at Reason with a huge smile on her face. "Oh, my God, Reason. That is wonderful news. That woman must really have healing hands."

"Yeah, she the goat. I knew she would be the one to do it. I've believed in her since the first day I met her, and now look, Ma, I'm actually getting better."

"This is wonderful, Reason. I couldn't be happier for you. I can't wait til you start back walking again. It's time for you to pop out and show niggas."

Reason burst out into laughter. "Calm down, Ma. Yo ass ain't Kendrick," Reason joked.

A few moments later, they were pulling back up to Reason's house.

Peaches helped Reason out the car, but this time, it was much easier. Reason was able to lift himself with his arms, and he was able to use his legs a little, which was enough help for Peaches to be able to get him out of the car and into his wheelchair.

"You see what I mean, Ma? Serenity getting me together." Reason smiled before wheeling himself to the door. Leaning over, he opened his front door before wheeling himself inside. When Peaches entered the home, she saw Kalahni sitting on the couch, now fully clothed. She way playing the PlayStation with Easton.

"Grandma!" Easton yelled, jumping up from the couch and running over to Peaches.

"Hey, Grandma big man! What you over there doing? Playing the game with yo mama? How you even know how to play?" Peaches asked.

"It's easy to play, and it's fun. You wanna play too? I can show you how."

"Yeah, big man, you can show me one game, then Grandma gotta go."

Easton grabbed Peaches' hand and led her to the couch. Taking the controller from Kalahni, Easton handed it to Peaches.

"Well, I guess this means you don't want to play with me anymore, huh?" Kalahni asked, faking a sad look.

"You can play again once Grandma is done, Mommy."

"Now you know you gon play with yo daddy after that. It's cool. I got new episodes of *The Circle* to watch on Netflix." Kalahni walked upstairs and headed to her room.

<hr>

Ace walked into Tori's house and instantly smelled the food that was cooking. Walking into the kitchen, he saw Tori in front of the stove.

"Damn, baby, you in here cookin' for a nigga?" Ace asked.

"You know it, baby."

Ace smiled, grabbing a beer from the fridge. He sat at Tori's kitchen table as he sipped from the can. Ace watched as Tori pulled golden brown chicken wings from hot oil and placed them on a plate. She opened the oven and pulled out a pan of macaroni and cheese before turning off the pot of greens on the stove.

"Dinner will be ready once the cornbread browns. Kilo should be here in a few minutes, then we can eat," Tori announced as she began setting the table. She'd set up this meeting for Ace and Kilo, so they could begin executing her plan. She was happy they both agreed to meet and work together. So, now all she had to do was let them know what she'd come up with.

Tori had just turned off her oven when her doorbell rang. Walking to the door, she opened it, already knowing it was Kilo. "What up doe, cuz? I see you got it smellin' good in here," Kilo greeted. He walked in the house and immediately eyed Ace as soon as he saw him. Kilo's guard was up, as he stared into the eyes of his enemy.

"We good?" Ace asked, noticing Kilo's animosity.

"I don't know. You tell me. You put a price on my head then killed my brother."

"Look, man, I ain't got shit to do with none of that shit. Reason put that hit out after you hit that lick on his spots."

"Fuck you talkin' bout hit a lick on Reason's spots? Who told you that?" Kilo wanted to know who was talking. Only two other people knew that he was in on the hits on Reason, and one of them was dead. He knew Chrome was the only other person that knew, but he needed to hear Ace say it.

"Look, man, I don't know. Word on the street was you was hittin' spots, then two of Reason's got hit. That shit was a no brainer. But that ain't my beef. That shit is between you and Reason," Ace announced, holding his hands up. Kilo nodded his head, letting Ace know he didn't have any smoke for him.

"Okay, now that we got all that out the way, we can all eat," Tori said, handing Ace and Kilo a plate. They all took their seats around Tori's table as she began discussing their plan.

"With all of us being able to benefit from taking Reason out, that needs to be our focus. Kilo, since you are the one trying to get revenge for Brick, you can take the shot. There are several ways we can do this. One is at his house. In my opinion, hitting him at home would be the easiest. Reason is his most vulnerable when he's at home."

"How the fuck you figure that shit, cuz? I know that nigga got hella security guarding his fuckin' house. That shit is a fuckin' death sentence," Kilo objected, quickly shaking his head.

"Security? That nigga ain't got no security. Reason a real street nigga; the only security he got is the pistols he has around the house. Tori is right though, hitting him at his house would be your best bet. Just let me know when you do. He got a two-year-old son that I don't want involved with any of this."

"Say less. All I needed to hear was there was no security. I promise you his lil man won't be harmed." Ace and Kilo talked for a few more minutes, and all Tori could do was smile. Her plan was going to work. If she used her cousin to take out Reason, Ace would be in position to take over the organization. *Ain't no way Peaches is going to be in the right mindset to run an organization after her only son is murdered.*

"I got a question though. I know why I want Reason dead, but why do you? I thought you and Reason was like brothers?" Kilo asked, confused.

"Shit changes. It's time for me to look out for me, and that's exactly what I'm going to do."

Kilo looked at Ace skeptically. There was something about the statement he'd just made that made Kilo look at him twice. *What if this is a set up? How the fuck this nigga sitting here with me planning out his best friend's demise? This another nigga that don't need to be trusted,* Kilo thought to himself. He made a mental note to have a private conversation with Tori.

Kilo stayed until dinner was over, then he left, leaving Ace and Tori to the rest of their night. Tori felt on top of the world with the plan she'd put together. She was showing Ace that she was on his side and willing to help him. She hoped this would prove her loyalty to him.

Over the next week, Reason went on with his life, not knowing the danger that was lurking in the shadows. Peaches was at his house every other day, taking him to his therapy sessions. Serenity had become a lifeline to Reason. With him depending on her for his strength, he knew she was the main reason he was doing so well, and he would be forever indebted to her. The journey to recovery had been long for Reason, but with Serenity by his side, it had been well worth it.

Reason was all smiles as he wheeled himself into the building, knowing that it was about to be a great day. With the feeling in his legs returning, Serenity let him know that he would be taking his first steps at their next session, and today was that session. It had been months since Reason had been able to walk, and he was eager to get out of his wheelchair.

"I want to come back there with you. You're about to take your first steps in months, and that's a big deal. I wanna see it. Hell, I might even record it." Peaches laughed.

"Don't be recordin' that shit, Ma. You gon' have me on there lookin' crazy. You can come back there though."

Peaches smiled before following Reason to one of the back rooms. A few moments later, Serenity entered the room, smiling from ear to ear. "Are you ready for today, Reason? I am so excited for you."

"Yeah, it's been a long time coming. But I know I owe all this to you. I probably wouldn't be about to take my first steps if I had any other PT."

"I am the best," Serenity joked.

Taking the oils from a shelf, she heated them before placing them onto the floor next to the mat. "You want me to call Shane, or you got it?"

"I got it. I think I can get myself out of the chair." With those words, Reason lifted himself up using the grab bar in front of him. Without him even noticing, Serenity was allowing him to take his first steps. She watched as Reason moved his feet inch by inch, using the bar as a crutch. Peaches, already realizing what was happening, placed her hand over her mouth in awe as she watched Reason. It wasn't until he'd sat down on that mat that he even knew what he'd done.

"Oh, my God, I walked." The shock was evident on his face.

"You did, and I'm so proud of you. Now let's get this massage in so that you can walk some more." Serenity smiled, sitting in from of Reason and pouring some oil into her hands. She rubbed it all over his legs and feet, same as she did at any other session. With Reason using the second part of the session to walk around the room, Peaches couldn't be prouder of her son as tears of joy streamed down her face.

This was the moment they'd all been waiting for since the accident, and it was finally here. Thanking Serenity, Peaches hugged her tightly, thanking her again for helping her son.

"Aww, Mrs. Alexander, you don't have to thank me. This is my job and something I love to do; however, I will say that Reason has been one of my favorite patients. His drive was unmatched, and I've never had anyone believe in my treatments as much as he did."

"Whatever it was, I think that we all need to celebrate. How about we all go out to dinner this weekend, my treat? I have to do something to show my appreciation."

Serenity smiled, agreeing to the invitation. She gave Reason her phone number, letting him know to text her the time and location. She normally didn't mix business with pleasure, but there was something different about Reason. Serenity wanted to get to know Reason aside from him being her patient.

After a few more moments of conversation, Reason and Peaches finally left Serenity's office. Peaches took Reason back home, wanting to be there when he showed Easton that he could walk. Peaches was extremely proud of her son and was happy that the worst was over. They pulled into Reason's driveway, and for the first time, there was no need to help him into his wheelchair. He got out of the car on his own and wheeled himself into the house. Kalahni was in the kitchen, cooking, and the delicious smell of food hit his nose as soon as he got inside the house. Easton, who was lying on the couch, watching TV, jumped up and ran to Reason as soon as he saw him.

"Daddy, can you take me for a ride in your chair?"

"Maybe later, but right now, I want to show you something. Why don't you go get Mommy and tell her to come here?" Reason smiled.

Easton agreed before running off, returning a few moments later with Kalahni.

"Hey, baby, what's up? Easton said you had something you wanted to show us?"

Without saying another word, Reason raised himself up from his wheelchair and stood to his feet. He began taking little steps as Peaches stood beside him, holding her arms up just in case Reason needed something to lean on.

"Daddy, you can walk again!" Easton cheered as he clapped his hands.

"Reason, this is such wonderful news. I'm so happy." Kalahni walked over to Reason, wrapping her arms around him. "This is right on time for Thanksgiving. Looks like our family has a lot to be thankful for this year," she continued.

"Yes, we do," Peaches agreed.

"I still have some work to do to strengthen my legs, but the hard part is over," Reason informed.

"Fuck that, we gon' celebrate yo accomplishment tonight. Let me go in here and finish cooking, so we can get this party started." Kalahni made her way to the kitchen. Grabbing her phone from the counter, she sent a text to Ace, letting him know the change in Reason's condition. Ace shot a text right back, asking Kalahni to call him. With Reason in the living room with Peaches and Easton, Kalahni walked outside to make a quick call to Ace.

"What the fuck you mean he walking again? How the fuck did that happen so fast?" Ace yelled into the phone as soon as he answered. He thought he had more time to see his plan through.

"Like for real walkin'. He came home from therapy today and stood up right in front of me. Why can't we just end this, Ace? I don't even want to be here." Kalahni was almost in tears. She was tired of living a lie and was ready for her family to be together.

"Calm down, baby. I promise you we are going to be together real soon. Matter fact, it's gon' be sooner than you think. I'ma hit you back tomorrow." Ace ended the call before Kalahni could say another word.

Ace pressed down on the gas in an effort to get to Tori's house as fast as he could. The news of Reason walking again was not what he'd expected to hear. Pulling up in front of Tori's house, he used his key to open the door before walking inside, calling out Tori's name as soon as he stepped inside. Tori ran down the stairs, hearing the urgency in Ace's voice.

"What's wrong, Ace?"

"This nigga can walk. The shit is over. It would have been easy for

Kilo to kill him when he was helpless. Kilo don't stand a chance with him now. He's about to get the organization. I already know." Ace was furious. Just when he thought they had the perfect plan, a wrench was thrown.

"Calm down, Ace. The plan can still work, and it will. Kilo is a shooter, no matter if that nigga is walking or not. Believe me, baby, Kilo got this," Tori assured.

Tori walked into the kitchen, grabbing Ace a beer and handing it to him. "We gon' get his ass, baby. All you gotta do is your part. If your part is handled, then we got it."

Ace nodded his head as he sipped his beer. He knew he would need to go see Peaches. He hadn't been over to see her in more than a week, and he knew it was time for him to up his game. Pulling out his phone, he shot a text to Peaches, letting her know that he wanted to see her later that night. She texted back several moments later, letting him know that she was busy, but he could come over tomorrow night. Ace agreed, knowing that would give him time to plan something nice for her.

After about an hour, Ace decided it was time for him to head home. There was a lot on his mind, and he needed some time to himself. Pulling into his driveway, he parked his car in his garage before heading into his house. Ace grabbed a beer from his fridge before making his way to the living room. He turned on his sixty-five-inch TV before sitting on his couch. *Man, all this shit can't be for nothing. Something gotta shake. Ain't no way this nigga bout to just take the company I've been working so hard to get.*

Ace knew he would have to put in some major work. He knew he needed a miracle if his plan was going to work. He sat in his living room for hours, thinking about what his next move was going to be.

***

The next morning, Reason woke up and for the first time in months, didn't need help getting into his wheelchair. Instead, he placed both of his feet onto the floor and stood up. He smiled as he was able to walk to the bathroom and handle his business without any assistance. Kalahni, who was already awake, was downstairs, cooking breakfast. Reason could hear the 90's R&B playing.

Once Reason was dressed, he made his way downstairs, still using his chair because falling down the stairs was the last thing he wanted. With Thanksgiving a week away, he wanted to take Kalahni to Home Goods, so she could decorate the house. Walking again gave Reason a lot to be thankful for, so he wanted to host Thanksgiving dinner at their house.

"Good morning, baby. I see you in here cooking up that good ass breakfast," Reason greeted as he entered the kitchen.

"Yeah, just something light. I got steak, eggs, home fries, and biscuits."

"Damn, baby, that shit sounds good as hell." Reason took his seat at the table while he watched Kalahni cut an onion. "I was thinking we should host Thanksgiving this year. We have a week to plan and decorate," Reason suggested.

Kalahni nodded her head in agreement, but in her mind, she prayed that she wouldn't be spending anymore holidays as Reason's woman. All she wanted was Ace. That was the man she had a family with, and he was the only man she wanted to be with.

"What you thinking about, baby?" Reason asked, wrapping his arms around Kalahni from behind and startling her from her thoughts.

"Oh, nothing. I'm just happy that you're doing better now. I know this was a trying journey for you, and I'm so glad it's over."

"It was trying for us all. That shit didn't just happen to me. It happened to you too. Your life changed after my accident the same as mine did. I just want you to know how much I appreciate you. You took care of me when I couldn't take care of myself, and I want you to know that I got you every day after this." Reason kissed Kalahni's neck softly. Her insides screamed for him to get off of her. Kalahni didn't want any other man besides Ace. Knowing she couldn't say those words, Kalahni smiled weakly.

Once she'd made everyone's plates, she went upstairs to bring Easton down for breakfast. She'd just made it down the stairs when the doorbell rang. Walking up to the door and looking out the peephole, Kalahni smiled when she saw Ace standing on the other side. She quickly opened the door and allowed him inside.

"What up doe, Kalahni? I just stopped by to see Reason."

"He's in the kitchen. We were just about to have breakfast. You hungry?"

"Yeah, I could eat." They made their way into the kitchen, and Ace couldn't believe his eyes when he saw Reason standing there, leaning up against the kitchen counter. Even though Kalahni had told him, Ace needed to see it with his own eyes.

"I know this not my nigga over there standing on his feet?" Ace announced, walking over to Reason.

"It's a miracle, ain't it? My PT really did her thing because none of us thought it would happen this fast."

"This is so dope, bro. We gon' have to celebrate this shit. Let me plan a party."

"No need, Ace. We gon' host Thanksgiving dinner here next Thursday, so we can celebrate then. After breakfast, I'ma take Kalahni to Home Goods so that she can get everything she needs to decorate the house. We all know how she loves that shit." Reason laughed.

"Can we go get ice cream after?" Easton chimed in.

"It's wintertime, lil man. No ice cream spots are open. But we can stop at the store and get some on the way home. How 'bout that?"

"Yayyyyy," Easton cheered.

Kalahni made Ace a plate, and they all sat around the table and ate breakfast. All she wanted was for Ace to save her. She wanted him to tell Reason that she was his and that he was taking her away, but when Ace opened his mouth, those words never left his lips. So, after breakfast, Reason, Kalahni, and Easton made their way to Home Goods, getting everything they needed to decorate their entire home for the holiday.

Chapter Eight

Ace got out the shower and dressed in a royal blue Dior button up shirt and a pair of black Dior slacks. Ace was Dior from head to toe as he sprayed himself with his Sauvage cologne. He'd made reservations at Peaches' favorite restaurant, and he knew he was going to give her some good dick before the end of the night. Grabbing the Gucci bag that housed the dress he'd bought for Peaches to wear and the bouquet of flowers he bought, he walked out the house.

Ace pulled up to Peaches' house about twenty minutes later. Walking up to the door, Ace rang the doorbell and waited for Peaches to answer. The door opened, and Peaches stood on the other side, wearing a silk nightgown. Ace walked inside the house and handed her the bouquet of red roses. Wrapping one arm around her waist, he pulled her close to him. He tried to kiss her, but she turned her head, forcing Ace's lips to land on her cheek.

"Damn, what's wrong with you? What I do?" Ace asked, confused.

"Nothing, I'm good. What's up with you?" Peaches lied.

"I been waiting to see you all day. I've missed you so much. I made reservations for dinner tonight and got you something to wear. Go get dressed," Ace spoke, handing Peaches the Gucci bag.

Peaches took the bag from Ace, but instead of going to get dressed, she stood there, looking at him. She had a lot she wanted to say but didn't know where to begin. Turning around and walking to her bedroom, she put the Gucci bag on her nightstand before pacing the floor. *This nigga around here thinkin' everybody fucking stupid.* Opening her nightstand drawer, she pulled out her gun before going back to her living room.

"Baby, why you not getting dressed? We got reservations in like an hour," Ace asked, looking over to Peaches. She was standing against the wall with her hands behind her back.

"You been fuckin' Kalahni?" she asked.

"Fuck you talking 'bout, Peaches? Stop playin' so much and go get dressed, baby. If we miss these reservations, yo ass gon' be eating McDonald's," Ace joked, walking closer to where Peaches stood.

"Don't fuckin' lie to me, nigga. I already know you fuckin' her so tell the truth!" Peaches had been waiting to confront Ace since the moment she saw him walking out of Reason's home when only Kalahni was there.

"Fuck I gotta lie for? You the only one I'm fuckin', Peaches," Ace shot back.

Before he could say another word, Peaches raised her gun and pointed it at him. "I saw yo ass leave their house the other day when Reason was at therapy. I know y'all fuckin'. What I don't understand is why you fuckin' me and her. What kinda weird ass shit you on, nigga?"

Ace couldn't believe this was happening. For the past three years, he'd been able to fuck Kalahni as much as he wanted to without anyone finding out. They had an entire baby together, and nobody knew. Now, Peaches was about to put a halt to his relationship and his plan. Ace knew he would have to lay shit on thick if he was going to get himself out of this one.

"Peaches, baby, put the gun down, so we can talk about this." Ace attempted to reason with her. He couldn't allow all his hard work to go to waste and hoped his gift of gab would get him out the hole he was in.

"I'm not lowerin' shit. You gon' tell me what the fuck is up. You fuckin me and Kalahni, and that's crazy. Nigga, you wanna be Reason or something? Cause that's what it's givin'." With those words, it was like a light bulb went off in her head. "Oh, my God, you been pressin' me to take over my organization. Yo ass is trying to be Reason, you weird muthafucka. If you think I'm 'bout to let this shit happen, you out yo fuckin' mind." Tears began streaming down her face as she realized she'd been played. She was nothing more than a pawn in Ace's fucked up game, and she was mad at herself for not seeing it sooner.

"When I tell Reason about this shit, he gon' fuck yo ass up!" Peaches yelled as she attempted to wipe her tears away.

Ace stood there, blood boiling, as he watched his plan crumble. *This can't be the end. I worked way too hard for this shit. And I got too much to lose if this shit don't work out in my favor.* He heard Peaches when she cocked the gun. Thinking strictly off of instinct, Ace rushed over to her, attempting to grab the gun. However, Peaches wasn't giving it up as easily as Ace would have liked, and they began tussling over the gun. As much as Peaches tried to fight, ultimately, her small frame was no match for Ace, and he slung her across the room. He didn't know how much force he'd actually used until he heard Peaches' head hit the corner of her marble coffee table before hitting the floor. Blood pooled underneath her, turning her white carpet a deep crimson.

Ace turned around, shocked at the sight, as he slowly walked over to her, calling out her name with each step he took. With his heart pounding, Ace slowly bent down, placing two fingers on Peaches' neck and checking her pulse. "Fuck!" Ace yelled out, realizing that Peaches didn't have a pulse. Sweat began building up under his arms and soaking his shirt. His heart beat fast as he stood to his feet, not knowing what to do.

"Fuck, fuck, fuck! Ace, yo dumb ass killed her. Man, what the fuck?!" Ace spoke aloud. He placed Peaches' gun into his pocket before running up to Peaches' room and grabbing the gift bag he'd given her. He didn't want anything left behind that would suggest him being at Peaches' house. He looked at Peaches' lifeless body one more time before walking out the door.

"Fuckkkk! What the fuck did you just do, nigga?" Ace asked himself as he drove. He couldn't believe what had just taken place. Peaches was dead, and he was the one that killed her. His palms were clammy as he gripped his steering wheel tightly, coming to a stop at a red light. He tried to take deep breaths and remain calm, but he knew he'd just fucked up. He had a plan, and Peaches getting killed was not part of it. *Shit, why the fuck did she have to find out I was fucking Kalahni? Everything was going good until this shit.* Ace made his way to Tori's house. He knew that if anyone could help him, it would be her. Ace knew if nothing else, Tori had his back.

He walked into her house, heart racing, screaming her name as he walked through the house.

"What's wrong?" Tori asked, running down the stairs, meeting Ace at the bottom. She looked at his panicked face and knew instantly that something wasn't right.

"I fucked up, and I mean really fucked up. And I don't know if it's any comin' back from this." Ace paced the floor as he ran his hands over his beard repeatedly.

"Baby, you're scaring me. Just tell me what's wrong. Whatever it is, we can figure out a way to get you out of it. Just tell me what happened."

Ace shook his head, knowing once he said the words out loud, the situation would become even more fucked up than it already was. However, he felt that telling Tori the truth would help the situation more than him telling anyone else. There was nothing left to do, so Ace told Tori what he'd done.

"I killed Peaches."

"You did what? How? When? Ace, the plan was to take out Reason, not Peaches. Fuck."

"I know. I fucked up. It was a mistake. I didn't mean for none of this shit to happen. She found out about the plan to take over, and she came at me with a gun. Before I knew it, she was on the ground, and blood was everywhere. You gotta help me, Tori."

"Okay, okay, just calm down. Let me think for a minute."

Ace walked into Tori's living room with her following behind him. They both took a seat on her couch before she spoke again.

"Did anyone see you walk in, or does anyone else know you were supposed to be at Peaches' house tonight?"

"Nah, don't nobody know shit about me and Peaches except you."

"Okay, good. It's a good thing that no one can put you at her house tonight. Reason would never think it's you anyway. I say just let the shit play out. Move regular, just like you would any other day, and never repeat this shit again."

"You think that's gon' work?"

"It's gon' have to. And if it don't, we'll cross that bridge when we get to it."

Reason woke up ready to get his day started. After getting dressed, he went down the stairs, still using the lift chair. Although he could walk, he still didn't trust himself walking down the stairs. So, until he was totally back to normal, he used the lift chair. Walking into the kitchen, he made himself a bagel and poured a glass of apple juice while he waited on Peaches. Both Kalahni and Easton were still asleep, and Reason didn't want to wake them. Once he was done with his breakfast, he washed his dishes before heading into the living room. He knew Peaches would be pulling up at any minute, so he scrolled through Netflix while he waited. He came across a series called *Catching Killers* and began watching. The series was so good that he didn't even notice how much time had gone by until the first episode was over.

Looking at the time and noticing he only had fifteen minutes before he had to be to his appointment, he placed a call to Peaches. When she didn't answer, Reason figured she was driving, and he turned on another episode.

"Peaches not here yet?" Kalahni asked, walking into the living room with Easton on her hip.

"Nah, and this ain't like her. She always early for every therapy appointment."

"Did you try calling her? Maybe she overslept."

"Peaches oversleeping when it comes to something for me? Come on now."

"Yeah, you right. If it's one thing Peach gonna do, that's be there for you. Maybe she on her way now. She might just be stuck in traffic," Kalahni suggested before walking into the kitchen.

She made Easton a bowl of cereal before making her way back out to the living room. She sat the bowl on Easton's Spider-Man kids' table and pulled out his chair.

"You want me to just take you to your appointment?" she asked, not knowing what else to do.

"Nah, I'ma wait on Peaches. She gotta be on her way."

When an hour passed with still no word from Peaches, Reason began to worry. He knew something had to be wrong because there was no way she would just stand him up. Grabbing his phone, he placed a call to Serenity's office to reschedule his appointment for the day.

"Baby, can you see if Michelle will watch Easton for a few today? I want you to take me over Peaches' house. Something don't feel right," Reason asked.

"Yeah, let me call her."

Moments later, they were leaving the house on their way to drop Easton off. In true Michelle fashion, she let her daughter know that she would need two hundred dollars if they wanted to leave Easton with her for the short time they'd asked for. Without hesitation, Reason reached into his pocket and pulled out a wad of bills, counting out a few before handing them to Michelle.

Once back in the car, Kalahni drove down the street, headed to Peaches'. Reason placed a few more calls to her, which all went unanswered. At this point, Reason's emotions were all over the place. The uneasy feeling in the pit of his stomach would not go away. However, when they pulled up and saw Peaches' car still in her driveway, Reason knew something was wrong. Rushing over to the door, Reason put the code in and opened it. The sight before him sent him to his knees before he could fully grasp what was going on.

"Maaaaaaa!" he yelled, crawling to her body. "Ma, please don't do this. Get up."

Kalahni walked in after him, eyes as wide as saucers, seeing Peaches lying on the floor. She didn't see all the blood underneath her until she got closer.

"Kalahni, call 911!" he pleaded, gently placing Peaches' head on his lap, trying to make her comfortable. He knew she was dead just by looking at her; however, he didn't want to believe it. Reason always thought his mother was the strongest person walking this earth. *Ain't no way she dead.*

By the time the police and ambulance arrived, it was about fifteen minutes later, and Reason was pissed it had taken them such a long time. When they walked in and felt for a pulse, there wasn't one. Her body had been cold for hours. Reason heard one of the officers make a call to the coroner's office, so they could come pick up the body, and he lost it. Tears began streaming down his face uncontrollably, and Kalahni didn't know what to do. She had never seen Reason cry in all the years they'd been together. She knew he was heartbroken; however, Kalahni was silently rejoicing. She knew that with Peaches dead, she could leave Reason with no repercussions.

"We are going to need the two of you to go outside as this is now a crime scene. I will have an officer come out and take statements from you both," one of the officers spoke, looking from Reason to Kalahni.

Reason stood there for several more seconds as he watched two men place his mother into a body bag. His entire world had just crashed around him, and Reason didn't know what would happen next. His mother had always been there, and the fact that she would no longer be just a phone call away was something that Reason couldn't grasp. *How the fuck can she be dead? Peaches can't fuckin' die. There's no way this shit is real.* Reason went through the first of seven stages of grief, and denial set in.

Chapter Nine

Two days had passed, and Reason had barely been able to get out of bed. It was like his legs had gone back limp, even though he still had feeling in them. He wished that his heart would go numb, and maybe then he wouldn't feel so much pain. Without his mother, Reason didn't know what to do. Peaches had always been there to help him through every hardship in his life. There was never a moment of sadness that Peaches didn't help bring him out of. Now, in the wake of her death, there was no one to bring him out of this.

"Daddy, are you okay?" Easton asked, walking into the room and up to the bed. "Mommy wants to know if you want something to eat," he continued.

"Nah, I'm not hungry right now," Reason replied, turning on his other side, so Easton wouldn't see the tears that were falling from his eyes.

"You wanna play *Mario* with me?" Easton, not knowing what was going on, was still his happy and cheerful self.

"Maybe later, big man. Right now, Daddy just wants to take a nap," Reason responded weakly.

"Okay, I'll come get you later so that we can play." Easton's optimism reminded Reason of Peaches. His heart ached, and he knew he could do nothing about it. There was nothing anyone could do or say to make him feel better. There was only one thing that would make Reason feel better, and that was having Peaches back. However, he knew in reality that would never happen. So, he chose to wallow in his own sorrows.

Reason lay in bed for a few more hours before Kalahni walked inside their room. She walked inside the bathroom and took a shower, never saying one word to Reason. When she was done, she walked into her closet to find something to wear. It was Saturday, and she didn't plan to stay in the house.

"Where you going?" Reason asked, lifting his head from his pillow. His eyes were red and puffy from all the crying he'd done.

"I'm going out for dinner and drinks with Tori. I can take Easton to my mom's house if you want me to."

"What you mean you going out? Kalahni, I just lost my mother."

"Umm, I know. I was there when you found her, remember? What that got to do with me going out?"

Reason couldn't believe his ears as he looked at Kalahni in shock. He had so many words to say but thought it best if he left it alone. With that, Kalahni finished getting dressed. Reason made sure to tell her to leave Easton with him before she walked out the door.

Getting up from the bed, Reason walked into the bathroom to wash his face and brush his teeth. He stood there, looking at himself in the mirror. "What the fuck am I supposed to do now? Mama, why you leave me like this? I'm a fucking orphan, a fucking orphan." The pain of his words hit him even harder than he thought.

"Daddy, what's wrong? Why you crying?" Easton's little voice startled Reason. He was trying his hardest not to let his son see him cry. Now, there he was, caught red handed.

Reason picked Easton up and walked him over to his bed. sitting Easton on his lap as he took a seat on his bed. "I'm crying because Grandma Peaches is not here with us anymore."

"Where is she, Daddy?"

"She's in Heaven with God," Reason replied in a low tone.

"Don't cry, Daddy. She'll be back," Easton said cheerfully, his two-year-old mind not being able to comprehend what death meant.

"No, she won't, big man. Once someone goes with God, they never come back." Reason tried his best to explain to Easton what was going on, but it was hard for him. At twenty-five years old, it was hard for him to understand, so he could only imagine what was going through Easton's mind.

"So, I'm never going to see her again? She can't play *Mario* with me?" Easton asked, becoming sad.

"No, big man. I'm sorry, but she can't."

"Can she still hear me if I talk to her?" Easton asked, looking up at Reason. By this time, Easton's eyes were filled with tears.

"Yes, she can hear you, but she can't answer you back."

Easton wrapped his tiny arms around Reason, hugging him as tightly as he could. "Don't cry, Daddy. Grandma wouldn't want us to be sad. She was never sad."

With those words, Reason wiped his tears, not believing that his two-year-old would be the one to bring him out of such a dark situation. Reason stood up from the bed with Easton still in his arms. "How 'bout we go play some *Mario*?" he suggested. They'd just made it down the stairs when his phone rang. Looking at it but not recognizing the number, Reason pressed the talk button.

"Hey, Reason, it's Serenity. I got your number from your chart. I was sitting here, looking for something to wear to dinner, when I realized y'all didn't give me a time or a place." Serenity laughed.

Reason didn't know what to say. He'd forgotten the promise Peaches made to Serenity to take her out to dinner. Reason looked over to Easton before stepping out of the room to speak with Serenity.

"My mom passed away the day before yesterday," he spoke softly. Saying the words out loud still felt unbelievable to Reason, but it was indeed reality.

"Oh, my God, Reason. I am so sorry. I had no idea. Is there anything I can do for you? What do you need?" Serenity asked genuinely.

"Thank you for asking, but it's nothing anyone can do for me."

Serenity heard the pain in his voice, and her heart went out to him, knowing the pain of losing a loved one all too well. Letting him know she was available to talk anytime he needed her, she ended the call.

Over the next few days, Reason had done all the planning for Peaches' funeral himself. Because she'd died a week before Thanksgiving, Reason was in a rush to plan the funeral, wanting to ensure Peaches was buried before the holiday. Thankfully for Reason, Ace did help out a little by ordering all the flower arrangements for the service. However, other than that, everything was left up to Reason. With him being her only child, Reason was able to plan the entire funeral in the few short days he had, having the service the Tuesday before Thanksgiving.

Reason dressed in an all-black, Balmain, three-piece suit before heading down the stairs to join Kalahni and Easton, who were already dressed. The black limo pulled up outside, and the three of them got in and made their way to the church.

About two hundred people came out to pay their respects to Peaches. The entire church had been decorated in Peaches' favorite colors — pink and gold. Reason, Easton, and Kalahni took their seats in the front row with Ace joining them. Reason sat there, numb, as he stared at the casket that housed Peaches' body. The preacher stepped to the podium and began saying a few words as the choir sang softly. The entire service was a blur as Reason watched from dark shades that hid his red eyes. When the service was over, Kalahni let Reason know she was going to take Easton home to change his clothes before going to the repast.

"You want me to come with you?"

"No, it's fine. It's only gonna take a minute, and we'll be right back," Kalahni assured.

Nodding his head, he watched as Kalahni and Easton walked out of the church. They got into the limo and pulled off.

"You need me to take you over to the repast?" Ace asked, walking over to Reason.

"Yeah, that would be cool. Kalahni just went home real quick to change Easton's clothes. Lil man was sick of being in that suit." Reason laughed, but Ace could still hear the hurt in his voice.

"I need to know who did this, man. There was no forced entry, so Peaches let whoever it was inside. So, I know it ain't Kilo. I don't give a fuck what them police say; this wasn't no fuckin' accident," Reason announced once they were inside of Ace's car.

"Man, you know I loved Peaches like my own mama. So, if that's what you think, then I'm with you," Ace lied, knowing Reason didn't suspect him at all. There was no reason to. To Reason's knowledge, Ace had no reason to be with Peaches alone.

"What's understood don't need to be explained. I already know."

<hr>

Reason had been at the repast for about an hour. He'd had so many people come up to him, extending their condolences, that he'd lost count. He'd been looking up at the clock every fifteen minutes as he waited for Kalahni and Easton to walk through the door. He knew they were the only two people that would keep him together. They were who would keep him strong in his time of weakness, and he needed them there.

One of the older women that attended Peaches' service prepared a plate of food before placing it on the table in front of Reason. "Here you go. I made you a plate just in case you wanted something to eat."

"Thank you." Reason nodded, looking down at the plateful of different items. He didn't have an appetite at all, but he appreciated her gesture. Standing up from his seat, Reason walked outside so that he could call Kalahni. He felt that her and Easton should have been there by now, and he wanted to know where she was.

Kalahni's phone rang several times before going to voicemail. He hung up before calling right back; this time, his call was sent directly to voicemail. "Come on, Kalahni, answer yo phone." Calling her phone once more, Reason became panicked when it went to voicemail again. *This is the same thing that happened when I called Peaches that day.* Rushing over to another limo that had driven his aunt and uncle to the funeral, he asked the driver to take him home, praying the entire way there that nothing had happened to Kalahni or Easton.

Pulling up to his home, he noticed the limo Kalahni and Easton had taken wasn't in front of the house. Surprisingly, Kalahni's Land Rover was also not in their driveway. *Maybe she told the limo to leave, and she drove her car to the repast,* Reason thought as he walked up to his door. Once opened, he walked inside the house, calling out for Kalahni and Easton. When neither of them answered, he rushed up the stairs, not even noticing he was using the stairs for the first time since the accident. When he made it inside Easton's room, his heart sank. He saw his dresser drawers open and empty. His closet door was also open without any of the many clothes that once hung there.

"What the fuck?" Reason rushed into the room he shared with Kalahni, only to find all her clothes, shoes, and purses were gone as well. Reason stood in the middle of the room, confused. That was until he saw a piece of paper that set on their bed. Walking over to it slowly, he picked it up before reading it.

Reason,

I know this might be a fucked-up time with you just losing yo mama and all, but this was the best time for me. With Peaches no longer here, I can finally live in my truth. And the truth is, I just don't want to be with you. I'm pregnant, and before you start having any ideas, it's not yours. Shit, neither is Easton for that matter. It's time for us to be a real family, and it's time Easton knows his real father. So, this is goodbye, Reason. Take care.

PART TWO

The Healing

Chapter Ten

A week had passed, and Reason still set inside his living room wearing the same suit he wore to his mother's funeral. He hadn't so much as showered since that day. The holiday had come and gone, and Reason had nothing to be thankful for. The depression that had set in didn't allow him to do anything other than sit there. A half empty bottle of tequila set atop of the coffee table in front of him, next to the empty bottle he'd already consumed. In just a few short moments, his life had spiraled out of control, and he didn't know what to do. For two years, he'd raised, nurtured, and loved a child that he'd now found out wasn't his. He couldn't understand how someone he'd loved so deeply could do something so cruel to him.

He wanted an explanation, a reason why she would even want to hurt him so deeply, but there were no answers. He'd tried calling Kalahni for days, and all of his calls went unanswered. Then, one day, he called only to find out she'd changed her number.

Sitting up from his couch, Reason grabbed the liquor bottle and took a huge gulp, enjoying the burn of the liquor as it eased down his throat. "How the fuck I ain't his daddy? I'm the only daddy he know!" His sadness quickly turned to anger as he stood to his feet.

"You the worst bitch ever, and my mama knew it. She tried to tell me, and I didn't fuckin' listen. Easton not my son though? How the fuck could that be? If I'm not his father, then who the fuck is?" Reason began throwing punches into the air, imagining Kalahni was standing there. Stumbling and tripping over his own two feet, Reason drunkenly fell to the ground. Out of breath and energy, he just laid on the floor. His doorbell chimed, and Reason didn't move. He didn't care who it was because there was nobody he wanted to talk to. The one person that he could talk to at this time was six feet under and never coming back.

After about five minutes of the nonstop chiming of the doorbell, Reason decided to answer it. Whoever it was wasn't going away, and he was tired of hearing the chiming. Standing to his feet, Reason made his way to the door, already annoyed by whoever it was coming to his house unannounced. He swung his door open, ready to go off on whoever was on the other side. He was surprised to see Serenity standing there.

"Hey, Reason. I'm sorry to just come over like this. I got your address from your file, and I hope that's okay. It's just... Well, you weren't answering your phone, and I was worried about you."

Reason opened the door wider, stepping to the side and allowing Serenity entry.

"How are you doing? I've been really worried about you. You haven't been to any of your appointments, and I know you're going through a lot with the passing of your mother, and I just want to let you know that I'm here for you," Serenity assured.

"Thank you, Serenity. I really appreciate you." Reason walked back into the living room, and Serenity followed behind him. She'd noticed Reason was wearing a suit and was about to ask him if he'd just come back from a formal event until she smelled the strong, musty odor coming from his body. That was quickly followed by the distinct smell of liquor. She looked around the living room, noticing the liquor bottles and blunt guts that were on the table.

"Reason, have you been sitting here since the funeral? When's the last time you showered?" Serenity asked.

"Yeah, this is what I wore. I ain't been feeling like doing nothing else."

Serenity could hear the pain in his voice as he spoke, and it hurt her heart. She wanted nothing more than to put a smile on his face, and she would try anything to do so. She watched as Reason picked up the liquor bottle and took a long drink before offering it to her.

"No, thank you," Serenity declined. "And from the looks of things, you don't need to be drinking any more either. Drinking is not going to bring her back, Reason." She softened her tone.

"She gone forever and so is everything I knew to be my life." Reason dropped his head low, running his hand across his face.

"I know it feels like that now, and I know nothing I can say is going to make you feel any better. Trust me. I know. I am so sorry you're going through this, but you can't just sit here wallowing in your own pain. Stress will kill you faster than anything."

"What the fuck do I have to live for?" Reason asked seriously, looking Serenity directly in the eyes.

Serenity felt her heart drop into her stomach as she saw the sadness in his eyes. "Nope, we not doing this. Get up." Serenity stood to her feet, grabbing Reason's hand and pulling him up. "Take me to your bathroom," she ordered.

Reason didn't object, walking up the stairs and taking Serenity up to his room and into the bathroom. She walked inside and began running water into the bathtub. Noticing a bottle of Molton Brown bubble bath, she poured some into the water. She walked back into his bedroom area and began going through the drawers until she found underwear, socks, a t-shirt, and a pair of gray sweatpants. She brought everything back to the bathroom and handed them to Reason.

"Get in the tub. I'll be downstairs when you're done."

Reason nodded his head as he watched Serenity walk out the room. She went down the stairs and began cleaning his living room. She could tell that Reason hadn't eaten anything, at least that day. So, when she was done cleaning, she went into the kitchen to find something to cook for him. Going through both his refrigerator and freezer and not finding anything, she opened the Door Dash app and ordered them both steak dinners from Starters. By the time Reason came back downstairs, Serenity was just finishing putting the food on their plates.

"I didn't know what you liked to eat, so I played it safe and got steaks. Is that good?" Serenity asked when Reason walked into the kitchen.

"You didn't have to do any of this. Thank you. And steak is my favorite."

They both sat at the table and ate dinner together. Reason hadn't noticed how hungry he was until he took his first bite. He couldn't remember the last time he'd eaten anything and knew if it wasn't for Serenity, he would have gone another day without eating.

"Thank you for all this, Serenity. You don't know what this means to me."

"Yes, I do. I know pain all too well. I felt the same way you do when my daughter's father passed away. Besides my grandmother, he was the only other person that I loved who I had to bury."

Reason stopped eating and looked up at Serenity. "How did he pass?"

"He was shot, shot right in front of me, and he died in my arms. I was six months pregnant with Scotland at the time. What was supposed to be the happiest time in my life quickly became the worst. I didn't want to live after that. And if it wasn't for Shane, I probably wouldn't be here today. He did what nobody else did and was able to pull me out of what could have been a deep depression. He reminded me that everything I was doing to my body, I was also doing to my baby because she was inside of me, feeling everything that I felt. After that, I realized I had to get my shit together."

Reason nodded his head. "Damn, I'm sorry that happened to you. I'm glad you had Shane there to help. Y'all must really be close."

"Shane is my best friend, and I'm glad he was there for me too. But I said all that to let you know that I'm going to be here for you. You overcame some physical pain that would have killed most people. And I'm going to make sure you overcome this emotional pain as well. You have a son you need to be strong for. He's two, right? He don't understand what's going on, and he lost his grandmother."

Reason hung his head low once more as tears threatened to fall from his eyes. The very mention of Easton saddened him, so much so that he didn't know what hurt him more, the loss of the mother that raised him from birth or the loss of a son he raised from birth.

"No, he didn't," Reason spoke softly.

"What do you mean?" Serenity was confused by Reason's response and thought she hadn't heard him correctly.

"He didn't lose his grandmother because Easton is not my son. I found that out the same day I buried my mother. I came home from the repast to an empty house and a letter telling me he wasn't mine, and they were going to be a family with his real father," Reason revealed.

Serenity had no words. She had no idea the amount of heartbreak Reason had been going through. Her heart went out to him, and she stood to her feet, walking over to Reason and wrapping her arms around him. She hugged him tightly, holding him close for several moments. Reason melted, not having a hug like this in such a long time. He was thankful for Serenity's presents and didn't realize how much he needed to talk to someone until now. He felt safe with Serenity. She'd seen him in his most vulnerable state, and she'd never treated him as less than. So, he knew this would be the same.

They continued to talk over dinner, and once Serenity washed the dishes, she let Reason know she had to go pick up her daughter but would call him the next day.

<hr>

Tori walked through her door after a long night at work. It was almost four in the morning, and all she wanted to do was take a shower and go to bed. It had been a little over a week since she'd spoken with Ace. She hated when he disappeared like this but knew it was only a matter of time before he came walking through her door.

Walking to her bathroom, she turned on the shower before stepping inside. The hot water soothed her body the moment it made contact. She lathered her body from head to toe, paying extra attention to her diamond between her thighs. She missed Ace tremendously and needed for him to come and make her feel good. So, once she was out the shower, she sent him a text that said just that. She stayed up for the next twenty minutes, waiting on him to text her back. When he didn't, she went to sleep.

Tori didn't wake up until after twelve the next afternoon. She checked her phone as soon as she opened her eyes to see if she had a missed text from Ace. She frowned when she realized there wasn't one. *Damn, where this nigga at?* Getting out of bed, she walked into her kitchen. Grabbing one of her pre-made strawberry parfaits, she took a seat on her couch before opening the Netflix app on her sixty-five-inch TV. She watched an episode of *Love is Blind* before picking up her phone and calling Ace. When he didn't answer, Tori shot him another text.

When her phone chimed a few seconds later, she thought it was Ace replying. Looking down at her phone, she was disappointed when she saw it was Kalahni asking if she wanted to go out to dinner at Kabuki. She replied back, letting her know that she would meet her at the restaurant at seven that night.

<hr>

Tori dressed in an olive-green, two-piece set, placing a cream sweater over it. Born in Roma was her scent of choice, and once she sprayed it, she was ready to go. When she arrived at the restaurant, Kalahni was already sitting at the table.

"Hey, girl," Tori greeted. Kalahni stood from her seat to hug Tori. "Girl, what's been up with you? I feel like I haven't saw you in forever," Tori continued, taking her seat at the table.

"I know, girl. It's been so much going on. I don't even know where to start."

"Damn, bitch, start at the beginning. Tell me everything," Tori encouraged.

"Well, me and Reason broke up. I'm pregnant and engaged!" Kalahni held up her hand, flashing her ring as she smiled from ear to ear."

Tori's mouth dropped open as she threw her head back. "Hold up, bitch. If you and Reason broke up, who the fuck are you pregnant by, and who are you marrying?"

"Okay, bitch, don't judge me when I tell you this, but I fell in love with Reason's best friend, Ace. Now, before you say anything, I didn't plan for it to be him. It just happened. Anyway, he's Easton's real father, and we both thought it would be best if we stopped the lying and told the truth. Well, the half-truth. I told Reason he wasn't Easton's father but never told him who his real father was."

Tori couldn't believe her ears. *What the fuck she mean she marrying Ace? And he's the father of her kids? What the fuck is she talking about?*

Ain't no way she bout to marry Ace. I was supposed to be his ride or die. Her heart instantly broke into a thousand pieces. Tears formed in her eyes as she fought like hell to keep them from falling down her cheeks.

"I hope I'm pregnant with a girl since we already have a boy. Bitch, you gon' have to help me pick out some baby names. I just can't believe I'm really about to get married. I'm really about to have my dream life," Kalahni gushed.

"Or mine." Tori spoke in a tone so low that Kalahni didn't hear what she'd said.

"Huh?" Kalahni asked.

"Girl, I said it's about time. I'm so happy for you, and I'm glad you're happy."

Tori let Kalahni know she needed to go to the bathroom, and she stood to her feet, holding in her tears as she rushed to the bathroom. Thankfully, her tears didn't fall until she got there. Pulling her phone from her purse, she called Ace, and unlike all the times before, this time, he answered.

"What up doe, my baby?"

"You tell me what the fuck is up. Why the fuck am I sitting here, about to have dinner with Kalahni, and she tells me that she pregnant and y'all fucking getting married? How the fuck can you do this to me, Ace?"

"Doing this to you? I ain't do shit to you, Tori. Fuck you even talking about? Me marrying Kalahni ain't got shit to do with you." Ace's words pierced her heart each time he spoke.

"If you don't want to fuck with me no more just because I'm marrying Kalahni, then that's on you. Just remember that was your decision, not mine. You told me you was my ride or die, so you supposed to be with me in any situation. Now you want to leave just because I'm getting married? That don't sound like a ride or die to me."

Tori's eyes filled with tears as he spoke, each word feeling like a different knife slashing through her skin. There was never a thought in her mind that Ace would play her. She thought that if she gave him what he needed, he would give her what she needed. Now, there she was, standing in the bathroom with her heart breaking into a million pieces.

Not wanting to hear anymore, Tori hung up in the middle of Ace speaking. She could no longer take the torment of his words. Going into her purse, she pulled out her concealer and fixed her makeup, not wanting Kalahni to know she'd been crying. She knew there was no way she would be able to stay and continue being in Kalahni's company, so she decided to leave. She walked right out the door, not telling Kalahni anything.

By the time Tori made it to her car, her eyes were filled with tears. She couldn't hold them in any longer as they poured down her face. *How could he just talk to me like he never even fuckin' cared? He treatin' me like I just wasn't shit to him. And he gon' fuckin' marry her? That bitch wasn't the key to gettin' Peaches' company. I was.* Tori was ready to give her all to Ace, and she thought he felt the same way, yet there he was, about to marry another.

There was nothing in the world that would have prepared Tori for the torture she was enduring. As she drove home with tear-filled eyes, she vowed to herself to get retaliation against Ace for everything he'd done to her. She thought they were building a relationship. He promised her that he would take care of her once he was in the top position. He told her the world would be theirs. Now, all Tori had was a broken heart and empty promises. *This what the fuck I get for trustin' that nigga anyway. I should have known his ass wasn't no fuckin' good. Only a snake ass nigga would set up his best friend. He gon' get his though, watch.*

Walking into her house, she walked straight to her kitchen and grabbed a bottle of wine and a glass. Her phone had been ringing since she'd left the restaurant, and she knew it was only one of two people, neither of them she wanted to talk to. Reaching into her purse, she saw she had two missed calls from Kalahni and six from Ace. Not calling either of them back, she placed a call to Kilo, asking him to come over, pouring herself a glass of wine as she waited. When she heard the knock on her door, she rushed to it, opened it, and allowed Kilo inside.

"What up doe, cuz?" Kilo asked, making his way to Tori's kitchen table. He pulled out a pouch, opening it and pulling out two green buds, and began breaking them down. Looking up at Tori, he could tell something was going on, and he wanted to know what it was.

"We not helping Ace no more. That shit is dead," Tori informed, taking a seat across from Kilo.

"I'm good with that. I wasn't trying to help him no way. My smoke is for the nigga that killed my brother. It never was about helping him." Kilo unraveled a Backwood before throwing the guts into the trash. He cut the paper into a perfect square before he placed the weed inside and twisted it up.

"What if the person responsible for that wasn't Reason?"

Kilo lit the blunt, taking a deep pull as he thought about what Tori just said. "Look, cuz, I don't know where this is going, but I told you from the beginning it was them both. Reason called the hit because I ran through his spots. But Ace, Ace was the one that took the shot. I know he was. That's just how that shit go. Reason gives the order, and Ace sees it through. Either way, they both are responsible. And they both need to go."

"Yeah, but what if we get them to kill each other so that you can keep your hands clean?"

"I don't give a fuck about getting my hands dirty. But what you got?"

Kilo didn't care how they went out, as long as they went out. Brick had nothing to do with what was going on, yet he was the one that was put six feet under. Someone had to pay for that, and in his eyes, it was the both of them. He was ready to lay his murder game down, and there was nothing that was going to stop him from doing so.

"I got some information about Ace that I know Reason don't know. This shit will fa'sho fuck him up." Tori leaned in closer before she continued. "Not only is he about to marry Kalahni, but they are about to have a baby together. And lil Easton, the son that Reason thought for all these years was his, is really Ace's child. I know when Reason finds that out, that shit gon' start a fuckin' war in the streets."

Kilo couldn't help but notice the sinister smile that spread across Tori's face. *Man, if she don't gone head on with this dumb ass internet shit. Who gives a fuck if Ace is fuckin' his bitch? This ain't even what I'm on. No matter what happens between them, they both gotta see me.* Kilo had one thing on his mind, and that was murder. So, he didn't understand why Tori was sitting in front of him telling him about the paternity of a child he didn't even know.

Kilo took a few more pulls from his blunt before he spoke again. "I don't give a fuck about none of that shit. Both them niggas bout to die, and that's my word. My brother will not die in vain. Both them niggas on borrowed time."

Tori nodded her head, knowing that once her cousin spoke that, his words were bond. There was no way she was going to be able to talk him into standing down, so she stopped trying. She'd gotten her cousin into enough shit trying to help Ace, so she was going to do everything in her power to keep Kilo's hands clean from here on out. They had already lost Brick, and if anything were to happen to Kilo because of her, she would never be able to forgive herself.

Serenity woke up and made her way into her bathroom. It was six in the morning, and the only thing that was on her mind was Reason. Her heart went out to him after everything he'd been through, and she wished there was some way she could make him feel better. *How the fuck could that bitch play him like that? Don't she know how many women wished they had a man like Reason? I swear, bitches just be dumb as hell.*

Turning on the shower, Serenity allowed the water to run a little while before stepping inside. She allowed the water to run down her body as she thought about the sadness that was in Reason's eyes when she saw him. He'd come so far in his healing, and the last thing Serenity wanted was for his depression to get the best of him and all his hard work go to waste. She knew the damage heartbreak could do to one's health all too well, and she didn't want Reason going down that rabbit hole.

Once Serenity was dressed for the day, she made her way down to the kitchen and began cooking breakfast, same as she did every morning. No matter how tired she was, she would always cook her daughter a hot breakfast before she dropped her off at daycare. Looking over at her clock, she wondered if it was too early to call Reason. Opting to send him a text, Serenity picked up her phone and began typing. *What do I even say?* Keeping it simple and just sending a good morning text, she put her phone down and continued to cook.

Not even two minutes later, her phone chimed, alerting Serenity that she'd received a text. She smiled once she saw it was from Reason, asking if she had time to talk. Instead of sending a text back, Serenity called Reason.

"Hey, Serenity. I see you're up early."

"Yeah, I'm getting ready for work. What you doing up?"

"Shit, I ain't been to sleep. Every time I close my eyes, I see my mama."

Serenity's heart instantly broke for him. She couldn't even imagine how he was feeling. *To lose your mother then find out that your son is really not your son, that bitch done fucked him up. He ain't never gonna be able to trust another woman.*

"You at home?" Serenity asked.

"Yeah, I'm here."

Serenity let Reason know she would be over once she dropped her daughter off at school. Ending the call and finishing up breakfast, she knew she needed to think of something to help get Reason out of his funk. Even though she had only known Reason for a couple of months, she felt drawn to him. Something in her just wouldn't allow him to go through this alone. So, once she and her daughter were finished eating, she helped Scotland get dressed, and they headed off to daycare.

Serenity pulled into Reason's driveway and got out her car, almost running to the door to knock on it. When Reason opened the door, Serenity's chest sank in. She looked into his eyes that were filled with sadness. Walking into his house, she sat her purse on the table and hugged him. She could feel he needed it as she squeezed him tighter. She felt his sorrows through their embrace.

Reason was thankful for Serenity more than she knew. In the short time they'd known each other, she'd been there for Reason through the hardest times of his life. It was like she was sent by God to help him through this time. Either way, Reason was happy she was there.

"Did you eat yet?" Serenity asked, breaking their embrace and looking into Reason's eyes.

"Nah, I ain't even hungry."

Serenity just shook her head. Already knowing there was no food in his fridge, she pulled her phone from her purse and opened the Door Dash app.

"Well, you gotta eat something. What you want?" Serenity asked, handing Reason her phone.

"Here you go. You just gon' make me eat, huh?"

"Hell yeah, fuck you thought?" Serenity joked.

"I guess just a breakfast from Coney, but I'ma pay for it. This the second time you came over and brought me food, and I don't want you thinkin' I'm some kind of bum ass nigga or something." Reason smiled, and it was the first time in weeks.

"Boy, shut up. I ain't thinking about money. I'm just trying to make sure you eat. I can't have you in here just skin and bones. That shit ain't cute."

"Still, if you gonna pay for breakfast, that means I owe you two meals."

"You don't owe me anything, Reason. I honestly just want you to be okay. And you not gonna have mental strength if you not gonna feed your body and gain physical strength."

Reason smiled, knowing what she said was true. "I know. It's just so hard. Every time I close my eyes, I see my mother's face. But every time I'm awake, I think about Easton. I go into his room, and all I see is the times I read him a book before bed or when I would play superhero with him. I just can't win."

Serenity just shook her head. She couldn't understand how any woman could hurt a man like Reason. In Serenity's eyes, he was a wonderful man, and she would have given anything to have someone like him in her life. Serenity hadn't even looked at another man since her daughter's father was murdered over three years ago, but Reason was different. Reason was the type of man that only came around once in a lifetime, and Serenity knew it.

Once she placed the order for Reason's food, she went and took a seat on the couch. "Come sit next to me."

Reason obliged without a word as he sat next to Serenity on the couch. He could feel her energy pulling him toward her, and it was a feeling that he'd never felt before. He looked up into her eyes and was amazed by her beauty. He'd known she was pretty, but something about looking into her eyes at that time made her the most beautiful girl in the world. *She must be who Prince was talkin' about when he wrote that song,* Reason thought to himself.

"I feel like you need to get out this house. You've been here every day since everything happened, and I think some fresh air would do you some good.”

“I just don’t feel like going anywhere. Being around people is not something I want to do right now.”

Serenity nodded in understanding. She understood exactly where Reason was coming from because she used to be in his shoes. However, she also knew those same four walls were no good to someone in his position. Serenity knew she needed to get him out the house, and she was going to do so. No matter what Reason said, there was no way she was going to let depression get the best of him. She had to be strong for him. She knew Reason wasn’t himself, so she felt she would have to be him for him. Her phone chimed, alerting her that her dasher was at the door, and she stood up, walking to it and retrieving the food. Serenity opened the bag and placed the food on the coffee table in front of him.

“Eat your food and then get dressed. We’re going out.”

“Serenity, I know you mean....”

“I don’t want to hear anything but okay.”

Reason looked up at Serenity, smirking. Chuckling a bit, he took a bite of his sausage link before nodding his head and saying, “Okay.” Reason didn’t take orders, but the look on Serenity’s face let him know she wouldn’t take no for an answer. So, once Reason was done eating, he headed up to his room to shower and get dressed.

“Where are we going?” Reason asked, walking back down the stairs.

“You’ll see. Come on.”

With that, the two of them walked out of the door, getting into Serenity’s Toyota Camry. They drove for several miles before they pulled up to a brick building. Serenity parked her car and opened her door.

“Let’s go.”

“Serenity, what the hell is this?” Reason laughed.

“It’s a rage room. I know with all of the feelings you’re feeling right now, anger has to be one of them. This is a way for you to get all that out. Come on. It’s gonna be fun.”

Serenity got out the car with Reason following her as they walked through the door of the building. There was a short, red haired, white woman that stood at the counter when they walked inside.

“Hello, and welcome to The Rage. How can I help you today?” the woman asked with a huge smile on her face.

“Hello,” Serenity greeted as she looked up at the different packages they could purchase for the activities they provided. "I would like Package B please."

"Okay, that will include one hour in one of our rage rooms. There are several objects inside that can be smashed. Once your hour is over, one of our team members will notify you. Please be sure to keep your protective gear on the entire time you are inside the room."

Serenity agreed, handing the woman her debit card before they were shown to their room. Just as the woman had informed, there were several items they could break — several televisions, computers, and other miscellaneous items, along with two sledgehammers.

"Serenity, where did you bring me?" Reason chuckled as he looked around the room.

"I told you it's a rage room. Now, put your goggles on so we can start breaking shit."

Reason obliged, placing the goggles over his eyes before grabbing one of the hammers. He walked over to one of the TVs, raising the hammer over his head before bringing it down hard onto the TV. The moment the TV shattered, Reason instantly felt relief. He began smashing several more items with Serenity doing the same.

After about an hour, they were back inside Serenity's car and heading back to Reason's house.

"Thank you for that, Serenity. I really needed that. Who knew a rage room would bring me so much joy?" Reason smiled.

"You're welcome. I'm glad I could be here to help."

"I know I owe you a meal after that. Are you free tonight for dinner?"

"I can be, as long as it's at a restaurant. If I have another dinner at your house, it's gon' be time to Netflix and chill after," Serenity joked.

"I mean, I did just pay my subscription." Reason laughed.

"Hahaha, you funny. But yeah, we can go out to dinner. I would like that."

"Cool, I'll make reservations for eight. So, I'll be to get you around seven fifteen if that's cool. Just text me your address."

Serenity nodded her head, letting Reason know she would be ready. Smiling, Reason got out her car and walked inside his house. The last time he'd been at a restaurant was with his mother, celebrating. The thought saddened him, but he was happy that he would have Serenity there with him this time.

<hr>

Serenity walked into her office building, greeting her secretary as she walked behind the desk. She walked into her office and took a seat at her desk just as Shane walked in.

"Well, ain't it nice of you to join us today."

"Good afternoon to you too, Shane. I'm glad you came in here; I actually have something I needed to talk to you about."

"What's up, Serenity?" Shane asked, taking a seat at her desk.

"Can you do me a favor and watch Scottie tonight for me? I'm going out to dinner."

"Dinner? What the hell I miss? Who you going out with, Miss Mamas?"

Serenity looked down and smiled before answering Shane. "I'm going to dinner with Reason."

"Reason?" Shane asked, perplexed. "You mean Reason Alexander? That fine ass patient of yours? I know you lying. I ain't heard you say shit bout a date or no man in years. Now you wanna step out with one of yo patients? And a fine ass patient at that. Bitch, you better not get pregnant tonight while you out ridin' his face. I mean, while you out to dinner." Shane pursed his lips, and they both laughed.

"Always the comedian, I see. I'll have you know that we are only going to dinner. There will be no sitting on faces tonight. He's going through a lot right now, and I really just want to be there for him. You know, the same way you were there for me." Serenity didn't give Shane any details, and she didn't have to. What was understood didn't need to be explained. Shane knew exactly how he was there for her and why.

Shane agreed to babysit, and they continued with their workday as usual. When Serenity arrived home, she prepared Scotland a quick dinner as she awaited Shane's arrival. Placing the pink Disney princess plate down on the kids' table in the kitchen, Serenity called Scotland to her meal before heading up to her room to find something to wear.

"Mommy, Uncle Shane is at the door," Scotland called out the moment she heard the doorbell ring.

Serenity ran down the stairs, opening the door and allowing Shane entry. "Hey, Miss Mamas, why ain't yo ass dressed yet?"

"I had to make Scottie dinner, and now I'm trying to figure out what I want to wear. I have a few pieces with tags still on them, but I don't know what I want to put on. I don't want to look too sexy. I mean, it's only our first date."

"Bitch, if you don't show that man why he needs to knock the cobwebs off that pussy, I will. Come on." Shane grabbed Serenity's hand, taking her up to her closet.

He immediately began going through the many garments that hung from black plastic hangers. Several moments later, he pulled out a black Dior mini dress that Serenity herself had forgotten was in her closet. He held it up to her chest and nodded his head. He paired the dress with a pair of black stockings before handing it to her.

"This the one right here. Now for shoes." Walking back into Serenity's walk-in closet, Shane walked over to her rack of shoes, taking a pair of classic, black Christian Louboutin pumps off the rack and handing them to Serenity.

"This is going to look good underneath your black, full length, mink coat." Shane smiled.

Serenity stood there in silence as Shane picked out her outfit from head to toe. "Okay, go take your shower and then we on to hair and makeup," Shane said with enthusiasm, clapping both hands together before placing them onto his chin.

"Thank you, but I think I got it from here."

Shane nodded his head, walking out of Serenity's room and closing the door behind him. Walking into her en-suite bathroom, she took a shower, making sure to use her vanilla scented body wash, knowing it would pair well with her fragrance of choice for the night. Once out the shower, she rubbed herself down with EOS vanilla cashmere body lotion. She turned on her Bluetooth speaker and went to her playlist on her phone as Ella Mai's voice filled her room. Walking back into her bedroom, she pulled a pair of black, lace thongs from her drawer and slid into them. There was no need for a bra with the dress Shane had chosen. Serenity's breasts sat up pretty, and she was very confident with her body. Walking back into her bathroom, Serenity applied her makeup before styling her hair. She kept it simple by flat ironing her curly tresses bone straight and parting it down the middle.

Looking down at her phone, she saw that it was already seven. With Reason due to be at her house in fifteen minutes, she knew she would have to hurry if she didn't want to keep him waiting. Once she was dressed, she placed a gold Cartier bracelet and necklace around her wrist and neck before spraying herself with Bianco Latte. She'd just slid her feet into her shoes when Shane knocked on Serenity's bedroom door to let her know Reason had arrived.

His eyes widened when he saw her. "Oh, my God, you look beautiful, Serenity. I feel like a proud house motha! Let me get a picture." Shane pulled his phone from his pocket as Serenity burst out into laughter.

"Boy, stop playing. I gotta go. I can't keep his fine ass waiting." She winked, grabbing her black Dior bag from her nightstand.

Serenity walked down her stairs to see Reason sitting on her couch, looking like every bit of the strong chocolate God he was. He unknowingly matched Serenity's fly with black Dior slacks and a black Dior button-up. He stood to his feet when he saw Serenity enter the living room.

"You look beautiful," Reason complimented, walking over to her and kissing her on her cheek.

"Thank you. You look good yourself, and you smell good."

"So do you. Are you ready to go?"

Just then, Scotland came running into the room. "Mommy, wait! I wanna give you a hug before you go."

Serenity bent down and hugged Scotland tightly. "Mommy will be back later. Make sure you're extra good for Uncle Shane."

"Okay, I will, Mommy. I promise."

Reason and Serenity walked out of the house and over to Reason's Land Rover. He opened the door for Serenity, helping her up into the car before closing the door. He walked around to the driver's seat and smiled when Serenity leaned over and opened his door for him. This was the first time he'd been out with anyone other than Kalahni in years. However, the nervousness he thought he would feel was nonexistent. He felt extremely comfortable around Serenity. It was as if they'd been knowing each other all their lives.

When they arrived at the restaurant about twenty minutes later, Reason got out the car, walking around to the passenger's side to open the door for Serenity. Taking her hand into his, they walked toward the door together. Once they were shown to their table, Reason pulled out Serenity's chair, making sure to be the perfect gentlemen to her. Serenity smiled, thanking him, before taking her seat. The waitress handed them both menus to look over before letting them know she would return shortly.

"What are you getting?" Serenity asked, looking over the menu.

"You've never been to Fishbone before?"

Serenity smiled shyly before shaking her head no.

"Don't worry. I got you. The gumbo here is delicious, and of course, they have the best seafood in Detroit. You can get whatever you want. Shit, if you want to order the whole menu just to try everything and see what you like, we can do that too. Matter fact, that's what we will do. How else are you going to know what you like if you don't try everything?"

Serenity smiled, not knowing what to say. Reason called the waitress over and let her know he was ready to order. Several moments later, several plates were brought out to them, filling their table. They tried everything with Serenity enjoying almost every dish. They sat and spoke for hours, enjoying each other's company.

Reason loved being around Serenity. Her aura seemed to heal him from heartbreak and bring light to his darkness. No matter how much sadness was in his heart, he couldn't help but smile when he was around her. Reason didn't want their night to end, so when they left the restaurant, he asked if she wanted to go over his house for a nightcap.

"I would, but Shane is at my house watching my daughter. We both have to work tomorrow, so I don't want to keep him out too late," she responded.

Reason nodded his head in understanding. Although he wished he could spend more time with her, he knew she had to get home.

"But I do have an early day tomorrow. So, if you want, we can do lunch."

"I would like that." Reason smiled.

When they pulled into Serenity's driveway, Reason got out his car to walk Serenity to her door. "I had a wonderful time with you tonight, Serenity, and I can't wait to see you tomorrow."

"I can't wait to see you either. Let's say around one?

"Cool. I'll be there to pick you up from your office at one."

Reason leaned in for an embrace, wrapping his arms around Serenity, telling her good night before watching her walk into her house. Reason's mind was filled with thoughts of Serenity on his drive home. Although he wasn't ready for their night to end just yet, he looked forward to seeing her the next day, so much so that when Reason walked inside his home, he went right to his closet to lay out what he would wear the next day.

<h1 style="text-align:center">Chapter Eleven</h1>

Serenity had just finished with her first patient of the day when she walked back into her office. Her phone chimed, alerting her of a text message. She beamed when she saw it was from Reason, letting her know that he couldn't wait for their lunch date. Sending him a text back, she placed her phone onto her desk.

"Girl, who you texting that got you in here smiling like this?" Shane asked, walking into Serenity's office.

Serenity burst out into laughter, realizing she'd been caught. "I'm texting Reason. We having lunch today. My last appointment is at noon, and I don't have to pick Scottie up from school until six, so today is the perfect day to..."

"To what? Spend time with yo man?" Shane cut her off.

"Boy, shut up. Reason is not my man. He's just..."

"Going through a lot. I already know." He cut her off again. "Girl, give that man some pussy. Trust me, you need some dick. And sex will do that man some good. Work out his muscles and help with his healing."

"Shane, get out my face. I'm not about to play with you." Serenity laughed. "It's not like that. He just cool. We vibe together and have a good time. Plus, with everything that he has going on, I want him to know that I'm here for him," she continued.

"Bitch, make that man yo man before somebody else gets him."

Serenity laughed, not taking what Shane was saying seriously. Although she found Reason attractive and often thought about him, she didn't want to push anything on him. *First, his mama dies, then his girl leaves him and tells him he's not the father of the child he's been raising for two years. That's a lot, and I don't need him rushing into anything he's not ready for. We are only friends.*

Reason was there to pick Serenity up from her job exactly at one. She walked up to him, greeting him with a hug. He was dressed casually in a pair of gray Nike Tech joggers and a white t-shirt. He wore a gold Cuban chain and a diamond stud in one ear. His hair was freshly cut and lined to perfection, and his Gucci Guilty cologne greeted Serenity before he did.

"How's your day going?" Serenity asked.

"It's better now that I see you."

Serenity smiled. "So, I know you're here to pick me up, but I don't want to leave my car here. I have to go get my daughter later. I'm sorry I made you come out your way. I don't know what I was thinking."

"It's all good, my baby. You can just follow me to the restaurant. No big deal. Let's go." Reason took Serenity's hand into his as he walked her to her car. Opening her door for her, she got in before he closed it.

"Just follow me. The restaurant is only about fifteen minutes from here," Reason informed.

Serenity nodded her head and watched Reason get into his car and pull out into traffic as she followed him. They made it to the restaurant exactly fifteen minutes later. They walked hand in hand to the door once more and was seated at their table. They placed their order and conversed as they waited on their food.

"I can't lie. I been ready to see you since I left you last night," Reason expressed, looking deeply in Serenity's eyes as he spoke the truth. Serenity had been the last thing on his mind when he went to sleep last night and the first thing on his mind when he woke up that morning.

"I wasn't going to say anything, but since you brought it up, I couldn't wait to see you either. I had a really good time with you last night."

"I hope that was the first of many."

"I hope so too." Serenity smiled. "I know it's still a few weeks away, but what are you doing for Christmas?"

"I don't have any plans now. Usually, we would host Christmas at my house. We would wake up early, so Easton could open all of his gifts. I would always have Christmas dinner catered because nobody wanted to be in the kitchen cooking all night. My mama would always come over, asking me why I didn't just ask her to cook when she knew damn well that she couldn't." Reason laughed. However, his laugh quickly turned to sadness as he realized he would be completely alone on Christmas day.

"Well, if you would like, you are welcomed to have Christmas dinner with me and my family. We're having dinner at my parents' house, and I would love for you to meet them."

Just like that, Reason's smile was back as he agreed to spend Christmas with Serenity and her family. They enjoyed their meal together while getting to know each other a little better. After Reason paid for the food, they said their goodbyes before going their separate ways.

Over the next several weeks, Reason and Serenity spoke every day. Reason cherished every conversation they had with it being the only time he genuinely smiled. With this being the first Christmas he would be spending without his mother and Easton, Reason couldn't help but to feel alone being inside an empty house. So, when Christmas day rolled around, he was happy to be spending it with Serenity and her family.

Reason arrived at Serenity's house at one on Christmas day. Taking the bags of Christmas gifts he'd purchased for both Serenity and Scotland, he jogged up Serenity's walkway before ringing her doorbell.

"Merry Christmas, Reason," Serenity greeted as she opened the door.

Reason smiled, admiring how beautiful she looked in the ankle length burgundy dress she wore. The dress fit her body so well, showing off her every curve. Her long hair was curled to perfection, and the perfume she wore drew Reason to her. He hugged her tightly as he took in her scent.

"Merry Christmas to you too. What perfume are you wearing? You smell amazing."

"Thank you!" Serenity smiled. "I mixed three different ones together. I have on Bright Crystal Noir, Good Girl, and Juliette Has a Gun, Not a Perfume. I love mixing my scents and coming up with different ones." She chuckled.

"Well, that's the one because you smell absolutely beautiful."

"Thank you!"

"These are for you and Scotland," Reason spoke, handing Serenity the gift bags before taking a seat on the couch.

"Thank you." Serenity placed both bags onto her coffee table and walked over to her Christmas tree. Bending down, she pulled two gifts from underneath it just as Scotland ran into the living room.

"Merry Christmas, Reason." She beamed. Running up to him, she showed him one of the many dolls she'd received for Christmas.

"Reason brought you a gift too, Scottie. Wasn't that nice of him?"

"More gifts? Yayyyyy!" Scotland cheered. "Thank you, Reason."

"You're welcome, Scotland."

"These are for you." Serenity handed Reason the two gift boxes before taking her seat next to him on the couch.

"Let baby girl open her gifts first." Reason placed the pink gift bag on the floor in front of Scotland. They watched as she reached inside and pulled out her first gift. It was a reborn baby that looked just like a real newborn. Scotland was so happy as she hugged the baby tightly. Reaching back into the bag, she pulled out several outfits, blankets, bottles, and pacifiers — all for her reborn baby.

"Thank you so much, Reason. This is my favorite baby of all time." She beamed, hugging the doll again.

"I'm glad you like her. It's your turn now," Reason informed, looking from Scotland to Serenity. He picked up the gold gift bag and handed it to her.

Reaching inside, Serenity pulled out three blue boxes. She smiled instantly, already knowing where the gifts were from. She opened the first box to see a gold lock necklace. She was so excited that she didn't know what to do. Serenity wrapped her arms around Reason, thanking him as she hugged him. When she opened the next box and saw the bangle to match, she hugged him once more. However, when she opened the last box and saw the earrings, she placed a kiss on Reason's lips.

"Thank you so much. These are beautiful, Reason. Now, it's your turn."

Serenity handed Reason the two boxes, and he unwrapped the first one. Inside was a bottle of Creed Aventis. Opening the next box, he saw a gold JBW watch with diamonds across the face. He smiled, leaning in and wrapping his arms around her as he thanked her.

They sat and talked for a few moments before Serenity informed them it was time to go. She put Scotland's coat, gloves, and hat on her before they all walked out the door, getting into Serenity's car and taking the drive to her parents' house.

They arrived about thirty minutes later, pulling into the driveway of the brick home. They all got out the car, and Serenity opened the door with Scotland walking into the house first.

"Mama, Daddy? We here," Serenity called out.

"Hey, baby girl. I'm just in the kitchen finishing up." Serenity's mother walked into the foyer. She was a beautiful peanut butter complected woman with short, salt and pepper hair. She wore a dark brown pantsuit with brown pumps. Her makeup was flawless, and Reason couldn't believe he was looking at Serenity's mother. The saying black don't crack fit well because he would have sworn she was Serenity's sister.

"Hey, Grandma. Merry Christmas. Where is Granddaddy?" Scotland asked, running up and hugging her grandmother.

"He's down in the basement watching the game. Why don't you go get him and let him know y'all here?"

They watched as Scotland ran off in search of her grandfather as Serenity introduced Reason to her mother.

"Ma, this Reason. Reason, this is my mother, Stephanie."

"It's nice to meet you," Reason greeted, extending his hand for her to shake.

"Well, isn't he handsome? Serenity, you did good with this one."

"Mama, stop. Reason and I are only friends."

"Yeah, right. Only man that's yo friend is Shane, and that's because he likes the same thing you like. If you bringing a man over here for Christmas dinner, I know it's wayyy more than friendship. You ain't gotta lie to kick it." Stephanie laughed.

"Mama, please stop. Is Shayla here yet?"

"Now you know your sister ain't coming nowhere on time. Shane not here either though. Plus, we still got about twenty minutes on dinner."

A few moments later, the doorbell was ringing, and Serenity walked over to open it. She smiled as she saw Shane and his boyfriend, Glover, standing on the other side.

"Merry Christmas!" she greeted, stepping to the side, so they could enter."

Both men hugged Serenity and her mother before Shane introduced Reason to Glover. Scotland returned, holding her grandfather's hand, as they both walked over to the crowd.

"Merry Christmas, Uncle Shane." Scotland ran over to Shane, hugging him. He reached into the bag he was holding and handed a box wrapped in pink wrapping paper to Scotland. He also reached inside the bag and handed a gift box to both Serenity and Stephanie. "Let me guess, Shayla ain't here yet?"

"You already know she gon' be late like always. I should have came late. That way, I would have been on time," Serenity joked. "Daddy, I want you to meet Reason. Reason, this is my daddy."

"It's nice to meet you, sir," Reason spoke, extending his hand.

"It's nice to meet you as well. I'm glad you could join us for Christmas dinner. You must really be special to my baby girl."

They all walked into the living room and placed the gifts Shane had gotten them underneath the Christmas tree until after dinner. They heard the door open before hearing Shayla call their names throughout the house.

"We in the living room, Shay," Serenity called out. A few moments later, Shayla was walking into the living room, joining the rest of the family.

"Okay, now that Shayla is here, we can finally eat," Stephanie announced, standing to her feet and walking into the dining room.

Everyone else followed behind her, taking their seats at the table. They all ate a delicious dinner and had great conversation before heading into the living room to open gifts.

Reason had a wonderful Christmas with Serenity's family. He seemed to fit right in with them, and he hoped this wouldn't be the last gathering he was invited to. At ten that night, Serenity decided it was time for them to go.

"Mommy, can I spend the night here? I wanna stay with Grandma and Granddaddy. Please, Mommy?"

"Well, if Grandma and Granddaddy say it's alright, then it's alright with me."

"They already said it was. Yayyyyy. Grandma, we gonna have so much fun. Can I do your makeup and your nails?"

"Sure, baby. We can have a whole beauty night. Then, we can eat leftovers and watch movies all day tomorrow." Stephanie agreed.

"Okay, Ma, let me know when you're ready for me to pick her up." Serenity kissed and hugged her family before she and Reason walked out the door.

"I'm sorry we stayed at my mother's house so long. I hope I didn't keep you out too late," Serenity apologized as she pulled into her driveway.

"Nah, I had a great time with yo family. I'm glad you invited me."

Serenity smiled before they both walked inside. They took off their coats and hung them in the closet before they both took a seat on the couch.

"Can I get you something to drink? A bottled water or something?" Serenity asked, walking toward the kitchen.

"Yeah, a bottled water would be great."

Serenity returned a few moments later, handing Reason a bottle of water. Their hands touched as he took the water from her, and the spark they both felt were undeniable. Serenity blushed, knowing he'd felt it the same as she did.

"I'm glad you decided to have Christmas dinner with my family and I," Serenity announced.

"I'm glad I was invited. I really had a good time. Your family was very welcoming to me, and I appreciated that. If it wasn't for you, I would have been sitting in my living room with a bottle of tequila and some Chinese food."

Reason scooted closer to Serenity, placing his hand to her face and softly caressing her cheek. Before Serenity could say another word, Reason leaned over, placing his lips onto Serenity's, parting her lips with his tongue. They kissed for several seconds before Serenity pulled back.

"Reason, I…"

"I'm sorry. That was too much. I didn't mean to invade your space. It's just…" Reason stopped, not knowing what to say as he dropped his head low in embarrassment.

"It's just what?" Serenity asked, placing two fingers under Reason's chin, pushing his head upward, so they could be eye to eye.

"You're always here. When I couldn't walk, you were here. You never looked at me as less than a man just because my legs didn't work. You are the one that helped me heal. When everyone left, you are the one still here, helping me heal again. This gotta mean something, right?"

"Reason, you have went through a lot in such a short time, and I don't want you doing something like this because you're searching for something else. I'm not saying I don't want this to happen. I'm just saying I want you to be sure if, and when, it does happen."

Reason looked at Serenity, slowly placing his hand on her face, gently caressing her soft skin. "This is what I've been searching for right here. And I would have never found you if I didn't have that accident. That's what I'm saying. You been here, Serenity. God put you here, and I've been feeling it since the first day I met you. I have always felt safe with you, and I didn't understand why until now."

Serenity didn't know what to say as she looked into Reason's eyes. She stared at him for several moments in an attempt to detect a lie. When she couldn't, she smiled. When Reason leaned in again to kiss her, she didn't push back. In fact, she grabbed his shirt, clutching it inside her hand, as she kissed him back passionately.

"Are you sure you ready for this cause it's no take backs?" Serenity whispered in between kisses.

"I don't do take backs," Reason replied, kissing her bottom lip once more.

Serenity looked into his eyes and saw nothing but the truth. She'd never mixed business with pleasure; however, Reason had Serenity breaking all her rules. She kissed his smooth lips, savoring the taste of his minty tongue. It had been years since she'd so much as kissed a man, and the way Reason was kissing her lips had a puddle forming between her legs. She wanted to stop him and didn't want to stop him all at the same time. She didn't want Reason to make a decision like this based on the pain he was feeling at the moment. She wanted to make sure he knew what he was getting himself into. *Fuck it, bitch, you need this shit.*

Reason pulled off his shirt and exposed his chiseled frame. He felt his manhood harden for the first time since his accident. He removed Serenity's dress, leaving her in nothing but her bra and panties, before running his hands over her soft skin, placing gentle kisses on her neck as he unhooked the black lace bra she wore. Her full C cup breasts sat pretty as Reason admired them for a moment before taking one brown nipple into his mouth.

"Damnnnn," Serenity whispered, throwing her head back in pleasure. She placed one hand on Reason's head, holding him to her breast. She licked her lips, enjoying the feeling of Reason's wet tongue. *Damn, if he sucking on my nipples like this, how good he gon' eat the pussy?*

As if on cue, Reason got up from the couch and took Serenity's hand before leading her up the stairs.

"Which room is yours?"

Serenity nodded her head toward the door, and they both walked inside. Reason laid Serenity on the bed, pulling her black lace panties over her full hips. Her freshly waxed pussy greeted him, and he dropped to his knees to taste her. Spreading her legs, Reason rested his head between her thighs. He licked her love button softly until her juices began running from her opening.

"Damnnnnnnn, Reasonnnn, I'm cumming!" Serenity screeched, holding Reason's head in place. Her sweet juices filled Reason's mouth, quenching his thirst. He continued to lick as Serenity's moans grew louder. He wanted her to cum again so that he could taste her sweet nectar once more. However, when Serenity attempted to pull his head away from her, he knew she couldn't take anymore. Standing to his feet, Reason took his pants off, his thick rod standing at attention. Serenity licked her lips as her mouth watered.

Sitting up, she scooted down on the bed. Grabbing Reason's ass cheeks, she pulled him closer to her. She opened her mouth, taking him in and wrapping her lips around his dick. Reason bit his bottom lip, and he threw his head back. "Shhhhit," he hissed.

Serenity wrapped one of her hands around his shaft, stroking him, as she licked the head of his dick. Reason's toes began to curl as he looked down at Serenity pleasing him. Feeling his climax approaching, Reason pulled himself from her mouth.

Grabbing his wallet from his pants pocket, Reason opened it and pulled out a condom. Taking out the condom, he placed it on his rock-hard dick before tossing the empty gold wrapper onto the floor.

Serenity laid back on the bed, legs wide open. Reason climbed on top of her, easing himself inside Serenity. Her tight wetness caused Reason to moan softly as soon as he entered her. Serenity wrapped her arms around Reason's body, holding him tightly as she opened her legs wider for him. Kissing and licking his neck, she moaned into his ear. "It feels so good, Reason."

Knowing that if he continued in this position he would surely cum prematurely, Reason stood to his feet and turned Serenity on her stomach, slapping her ass as he watched it jiggle. Serenity got on all fours, arching her back while she waited for Reason to enter her. Grabbing her hips and pulling her toward him, Reason placed all nine inches of his thick manhood inside her. Matching his rhythm, she threw her ass back, calling out for Reason to fuck her harder. Reason obliged, pulling Serenity's hands behind her back, holding them both as he pumped harder.

"Yesssssss, Reason! That's it, just like that. Make me cum again!"

"You say you like that shit, baby? Say that shit again. Tell Daddy you like that shit."

"I love this shit, Daddy. This dick is soooo good."

Letting go of Serenity's arms, he placed his hand around her neck and pulled her up to him. With her back to his chest, Reason gently turned Serenity's neck, kissing her passionately, his tongue massaged hers as he pumped in and out of her wetness. "You feel so good," Reason whispered into Serenity's ear.

She bit her bottom lip as his lips touched her earlobe with each one of his words. Moving his hand from the front of her neck to the back, he pushed Serenity's face down into the mattress, forcing her ass straight up in the air. Picking up his speed, he slapped her ass as it bounced off of him. He knew his nut was nearing. It had been so long since he'd felt the inside of a woman, and Serenity's wetness was too good for him to hold off any longer. He heard Serenity's moans grow louder and knew that her climax was nearing as well.

"Reason, I'm cuummming!"

With those words, Reason let his seed spill into the condom as they both came at the same time. Breathing heavily, they both passed out on the bed. Serenity laid there for several seconds, looking at Reason in amazement. Getting out of bed, Reason walked into her en-suite bathroom to dispose of the condom and clean himself up. Serenity walked inside the moment Reason came out, cleaning herself before getting back into bed. She laid her head on Reason's chest, and he cuddled her tightly as they fell asleep.

Ace drove through the city streets on his way to every dope spot Peaches owned, picking up all the money that was there. He planned on moving Kalahni and their son out to Lansing. He knew that once he staked his claim as the new head of Peaches' organization, there would be a target on his back. He hadn't spoken to Reason since the funeral and didn't plan to. As far as he knew, Reason hadn't been on the block at all to even collect any money or provide any work, and somebody had to do it.

Ace walked into Peaches' spot in Southwest. It was the spot that Chrome ran, an auto body shop that specialized in more than just oil changes. Walking inside, he saw Chrome through the huge window in his office talking on the phone. He seemed to be in the middle of a heated conversation; however, Ace could have cared less as he walked into Chrome's office, interrupting his conversation.

"I need to talk to you. Now," Ace ordered, taking a seat in one of the two chairs opposite Chrome's desk.

"Let me call you back," Chrome spoke into the phone, never taking his eyes off Ace. "What's up doe?" Chrome asked, unsure of what this unexpected visit was about.

"I'm here to pick up the money from the last drop. With Peaches gone, I will be taking over from here on out. That means you are to answer to me now and no one else.”

“What you mean? Where is Reason? I knew with Peaches passing away, shit would be different, but I always thought Reason would be the one taking over.”

“Well, he’s not, and it seems to me that you asking the wrong questions. I’m here for my cash and to let you know the chain of command from here on out. Reason is out, and that’s just what it is. I got other spots to get to, so just bag my shit up.” Ace wasn’t there to explain anything. He was there to take what was his. Although Peaches’ death threw a wrench in his original plan, he was quickly able to think of another. He would collect all the money he could before moving his family out to Lansing. He would only come back out to the city twice a month to reup anyone who needed it and to collect his money.

Chrome walked over to the safe, opening it and placing the stacks of money that was inside into a black backpack before handing it off to Ace. Chrome didn’t say a word, already knowing that something wasn’t right. He placed a call to Kilo the moment Ace walked out of the auto shop.

“Bro, we need to meet,” Chrome spoke into the phone.

“Meet me at that spot in Eastpoint.”

<h1 style="text-align:center">Chapter Twelve</h1>

Chrome pulled into the driveway of the small ranch style home where Kilo's sister lived. Not many people knew about his sister, Bubblegum; most only knew about Kilo's twin brother, Brick. Kilo kept it that way for times like this. When he needed a place to lay low, Bubblegum's house would be the last place anyone would look. Chrome knocked on the door, walking inside once Bubblegum answered.

"What up, Bubblegum? How you been?"

"I've been okay. You know how that shit go. Brick is the second sibling me and Kilo had to bury. This why we keep this family shit a secret because you just never know who gunnin' for who. But it is what it is. What about you? How you holdin' up?"

"Yeah, I feel you. I never really understood that shit til now. Shit really crazy out here in them streets. But one thing about it, the Browns gon' ride for each other. I'm good though, considering. I just need to get up with Kilo for a bit."

"He's down in the basement. You can go down there."

Chrome nodded before making his way down the basement steps. Kilo was sitting on the couch, rolling a blunt. He greeted Chrome when he saw him, telling him to take a seat next to him.

"Dawg, something is going on. Why the hell Ace just came to the spot to pick up the money and drop some more shit off? That nigga told me he was the nigga runnin' everything and that I should answer only to him. Does Reason know this shit?"

"Who gives a fuck what that nigga knows?" Kilo lit his blunt, taking several pulls before handing it to Chrome.

"What's yo beef with Reason? I thought y'all was cool?" Chrome looked over at Kilo.

"You already know. And since we on the subject, I see you was the one that told Ace that we hit Reason's spot? The more and more I think about it, nigga, how ain't it a hit on yo head too?" Kilo cut his eyes at Chrome. He would have never thought Chrome would become a snake, but as he thought about everything and the way it played out, he knew it couldn't have been anyone else.

"Bro, are you serious? What you mean I told Ace? He already knew. You don't remember I told y'all everything we got had to be split four ways? Well, who do you think that other person was? Ace set up them hits, telling me it was how we could get more money than what Reason and Peaches was paying us. Next thing I know, Brick was dead, and you was running."

Chrome shook his head as everything unfolded right before his eyes. He couldn't believe he'd been a pawn in Ace's game without even knowing. He blew out a cloud of smoke before he continued. "I think that bullet was meant for Brick, and it's another one that's meant for you. I can't lie. I told Brick about Ace being the one who planned the hits. I was supposed to be the only one that knew Ace was behind it, but I told Brick. And maybe that makes this my fault. But Brick felt the money shouldn't be getting split equally four ways. He felt since we were the ones in the field getting dirty, then we should get more money. Next think I know, Brick is dead. I didn't even put two and two together until I heard in the streets that I was the one that supposedly pulled the trigger. I'm sure Ace put that shit out in the streets too."

Kilo, shocked by what he was hearing, could only shake his head. He'd never heard anyone say Chrome pulled that trigger. It was all starting to make sense to him. Ace had Reason call the hit to take the heat off him. *Shit, for all I know, Brick could have been dead before the hit was even placed on my head. Tori might have been able to protect that nigga for a minute, but she damn sure can't no more. It's time for me to go with my own plan.*

"What the fuck Ace got against Reason? Them niggas supposed to be brothers," Kilo asked, looking over to Chrome.

"I don't know, but that nigga is a fucking snake. And you know what we do to snakes."

"Chop the fuckin' heads off," they both spoke in unison.

That was all Kilo needed to hear. He trusted Chrome's word over anyone else's in the crew. You see, what nobody knew was that Chrome was Kilo's cousin and Tori's younger brother. There was no way Chrome would have turned on his family, and they all knew that. Since birth, they were all taught to stick together with their mothers being the Brown sisters, known across the entire state of Georgia. They'd made so much money throughout the state that everyone knew who they were. They ran the south as the top drug distributors of their time. That was until a man named Cannon came along and took Georgia by storm. He came with a plan to be the only one moving weight in the south, and his ruthlessness would make sure he accomplished just that. When he began killing the top dealers in all the cities in Georgia, the sisters knew it was only a matter of time before they would be found and slaughtered.

With that, they packed their children up in the middle of the night and took the long drive up north. They lived in several different northern states before finally settling in Detroit, Michigan. However, since Peaches was already running the city and they didn't need to make any more enemies, they decided it was best if they befriended Peaches and began working with her. In return, not only were they paid very well, but they also had full protection from Cannon.

That was until one night years later when they thought all had been forgotten. Their usual security guard was off due to his wife going into labor two weeks early. All the children were gone with only Chrome being at the home. He was the youngest and was only four years old at the time. The sisters were sent over another guard to watch their house, but the guard was never seen. That night, someone broke into the home and killed the Brown sisters. That next morning, Kilo and Brick found their mother and aunt murdered in the house. From that moment on, they vowed to always keep each other safe.

Kilo dapped Chrome up before watching him walk back up the stairs. Chrome had come in to shine some new light on a dark situation, and Kilo knew exactly what he had to do next. With that, he grabbed his keys and jogged up the steps, making his way to Tori's house.

Chapter Thirteen

Tori sat on her couch with a glass of wine in her hand. It had been several days, and she still hadn't spoken to either Ace or Kalahni. They had both called her several times, but she had no desire to speak with either of them. She sipped from the glass, thinking about how she could fuck both of their lives up. Her phone rang, and she ignored it, not wanting to be bothered with anyone. However, when her phone rang again right after, she grabbed it, looking down at her screen. Seeing it was Kilo, she swiped the talk button.

"What up doe, cousin?" she greeted.

"Open your door. I'm pulling into your driveway right now."

Tori sat her glass down on her coffee table and stood to her feet. She opened the door, and Kilo rushed into her house.

"Call that nigga, Ace, over here right now! That's a dead nigga!" Kilo yelled.

"I can't call him. I don't fuck with him no more. You already know that shit. What the fuck happened now?"

"That nigga is the one that killed Brick. Now he got niggas in the hood thinking Chrome pulled that trigger."

"Chrome? What does he have to do with any of this?"

"Nothing, but that nigga, Ace, wants people to think he does. That's how I know that nigga was the one to pull that trigger. He was the one that set up the licks anyway. That's something else that I just found out. I want that nigga dead like yesterday. Give me his address, some spots he be at, something. This nigga getting up outta here."

"He trying to put this shit on Chrome?" Tori's blood boiled hearing the news about her little brother. It was one thing for Ace to come for Kilo. She knew speaking with Ace would stop that beef. But the fact that Ace was spreading the rumor that Chrome killed Brick made Tori furious. She instantly knew she would have to put a stop to this, even if it meant putting a permeant end to Ace all together.

"Yeah, Chrome let me know the streets been talking today. Chrome would never let no harm come to Brick, but Ace don't know that shit. We keep this family shit out the streets."

"I don't know his address. I know he moved recently. But I think I might be able to get it."

Tori took in everything Kilo was saying to her. She knew exactly what she had to do, and now nothing was stopping her. Any love she'd felt for Ace was now gone, and it had been replaced with abhorrence. The mere thought of the way she allowed that man to lay with her now turned her stomach. It was her time to show Ace who not to play with, and that was exactly what she was going to do.

"I got this one. Let me handle this shit," Tori voiced, walking into the living room and grabbing her glass of wine.

"What you mean you gon' handle it? That nigga got to go. If that ain't what you doin' then you not handlin' shit. I'm gon' kill this nigga. Just get me that address, Tori."

"No, you not gon' do shit. I got this. Just give me a couple days. That nigga needs to suffer, and I want to watch that shit happen. I just need some time. If that nigga not dead by the end of the month, then you can do what you want with him."

Kilo nodded his head in agreement, letting Tori know he would go along with her plan for the time being. Honestly, he wanted to see how Tori was really going to handle this. He knew Ace had hurt Tori, and he knew the type of pressure a scorned woman could apply. So, maybe, the type of pain Tori could bring him might be better than the gunplay Kilo would come with. Although he truly wanted revenge for Brick, he would allow Tori to do her damage first. He sat down, conversing with Tori for several more moments before walking out the door.

It had almost been a week since Christmas, and Reason and Serenity hadn't let a day go by without them seeing each other. Serenity was the first thing on Reason's mind when he woke up every morning and the last thing on his mind at night. Reason's feelings for Serenity were growing by the day, and he couldn't wait to see what the future held for the two of them.

It was New Year's Eve, and Reason and Serenity agreed they would spend it together at Serenity's house. He'd grabbed two bottles of champagne from the liquor store down the street from his home and made his way to Serenity. Although he'd just been with her the day before, he was eager to see her again. The joy he felt when he was with Serenity was a high he'd never felt before. He craved that shit like a crackhead, and Serenity was an addiction he never wanted to let go.

Pulling into her driveway, Reason got out the car before walking to her door. Serenity answered, greeting him with a kiss as he walked inside. He smiled, looking at the setup she' made in her living room. She'd pushed all her couches to the back of her living room and placed a palette on the floor in front of her TV. On the side of the palette was a small table with a host of snacks and drinks. In the far-right corner of the living room was a larger table complete with a loaded taco bar. There was also a painting station in another corner, complete with three easels, several different colors of paint, three canvases, and a host of brushes. Reason smiled, feeling this would be a wonderful way to bring in the new year.

"Reasonnn!" Scotland screamed, rushing into the living room and hugging Reason's leg tightly. Reason smiled before picking her up.

"Hey, Scottie. How you doing, pretty girl?"

"Good. Mommy said we gonna have fun tonight. She said I can paint whatever I want over there." Scotland pointed to the painting station.

"Yeah, we are gonna have fun. I see Mommy got a whole set up going on. This is really dope."

"I'm glad you like it. I got the idea from Pinterest. I think it came out cute too."

Reason put Scotland down before taking off his shoes and walking over to the palette and taking a seat. "What's the first movie?"

"*Princess and the Frog*!" Scotland yelled, running over to the palette and sitting next to Reason.

"Well, I guess that settles that. *Princess and the Frog* it is." Serenity laughed, sitting on the palette next to them both. Opening the Disney+ app, Serenity turned on *Princess and the Frog*. Serenity took a few snacks from the tray before placing them on the palette in front of them. They watched the movie together with Scotland singing every song.

When the movie was over, they ate tacos before sitting down again to watch the next movie. Reason felt good about making these memories with Serenity and Scotland and hoped this would be the first of many. They watched *Moana* before they decided it was time to start painting. It was almost eight that evening, and Serenity knew that Scotland wanted to paint before her bedtime.

Serenity walked to the kitchen and placed water into three paper cups before bringing them back into the living room. She opened the paint and squeezed a bit of each color onto three paper plates. They each painted a canvas before Serenity took Scotland upstairs to get cleaned up and ready for bed.

"She's finally asleep. Now it's just us," Serenity informed, walking back down to the living room.

"Cool, I poured us a couple of glasses of champagne. You wanna watch a movie until it's time to see the ball drop?"

"Yeah, we can watch anything you want to since you set through two Disney movies."

"Hey now, *Princess and the Frog* is my shit. That movie got soul. Hands down the best Disney movie ever made."

"Okay, you telling the truth with that one. Best soundtrack ever." Serenity laughed.

They cuddled up on the palette, sipping from champagne flutes, as they scrolled through Netflix. Reason finally settled on a movie, turning on *John Wick*. Serenity had never seen the movie before, and she enjoyed the action-packed film. When it was over, they watched the ball drop, and for the first time in years, Serenity had someone to kiss at midnight. They ended the night in Serenity's bed making love.

It was the Friday after New Years, and Serenity informed Reason that she wanted to go to karaoke. Even though Reason wasn't a huge fan of karaoke, he was going to give Serenity what she'd asked for. He arrived at Serenity's house around eight thirty that night. Pulling into her driveway and walking up to her door, Reason rang her doorbell as he waited for her to answer. To his surprise, Shane answered the door.

"Hey, Reason, nice to see you. Serenity will be down in a few."

"What's up, Shane? Ain't no thang." Reason walked inside and took a seat on the couch next to Scotland. She was sitting down, watching an episode of *My Little Pony*.

"Hey, Scottie, how's the prettiest little girl in the entire world doing? Can I watch TV with you while I wait on your mother?"

"I'm good, just watching *My Little Pony*. Yeah, you can sit here if you want to. But you have to hold Lizzy." She smiled, placing a baby doll in Reason's hands. "That's where Uncle Shane was sitting, and he was holding Lizzy, so she could see the TV. If you gonna sit there now, then you gotta hold her."

Reason chuckled a bit before placing the baby doll upward in his arms, allowing her to face the TV. Scotland smiled before turning back to her show. A few moments later, Serenity walked down the stairs. She was wearing a pair of black leggings, a white Off White hoodie, and a pair of panda Dunks. Her hair was neatly brushed in a low ponytail, and she wore a pair of small gold hoop earrings. Reason smiled as he looked up at her. He placed the baby doll on the couch next to Scotland before standing to his feet.

"You look beautiful."

"Thank you. I see she got you helping Lizzy watch *My Little Pony*." Serenity laughed.

"I didn't mind one bit. We was just chillin' while I waited. Are you ready to go?"

Serenity nodded her head before walking over to Scotland and kissing her on the cheek, letting her know she would be back later. They walked to the car before pulling out her driveway and heading to the bar.

"I can't believe I let you drag me to karaoke. I hope you don't think

I'm about to get up here and start singing in front of people," Reason spoke as they walked into the bar.

"You are though. That's the whole point of karaoke. It's gonna be fun. Once you get a couple of drinks in your system, you not gonna even notice all these people."

"Whatever you say."

They took their seats at a table before looking over the menu. After placing an order for hot wings and a few drinks, they looked over the selection of songs they could choose to sing.

"You wanna sing a song together or do them separately?" Serenity asked, looking over at Reason.

"We can sing a duet. What song you got in mind?"

Serenity thought for a moment before letting him know she wanted to sing *Fire and Desire* by the late Rick James and Teena Marie. Reason agreed, and Serenity walked over to the sign-in sheet to write their names and the song they would be singing. The moment their names were called to the stage, Reason instantly regretted agreeing to bring Serenity to karaoke. Serenity grabbed his hand, damn near pulling him on stage, and handed him a mic.

The song began to play, and the words started to appear on the screen in front of them. *Why the fuck did I agree to this song? I forgot Rick did all this damn talking in the beginning,* Reason thought to himself, placing the mic to his lips and beginning to recite the words on the screen before busting out into his full-on Rick James' singing voice. Serenity looked over at him, not knowing Reason could sing as well as he could. When it was Serenity's turn, she knew it was time to blow the house down, putting on an entire concert at the karaoke bar. They both got off the stage, laughing, and Reason was ready to sign them up for the next song.

Sitting back at the table, they ate a few hot wings and sipped from their drinks before finding the next song they were going to sing. Since Serenity had chosen the first song, Reason picked the next one. It was Chris Brown and Rihanna's song, *Birthday Cake*. After taking the shots they ordered, they were called back up to the stage. They sang song after song until the bar was ready to close.

Serenity and Reason laughed the entire ride back to Serenity's house. They'd both had a good time, and Reason was surprised he was able to open up enough to get on stage in front of an entire bar. That was the way Serenity made him feel though, fearless as if he could do anything. When they got back to Serenity's house, Reason got out the car before walking over to the passenger's side and opening Serenity's door for her.

It was after two in the morning, and neither of them had expected they would be out as late as they were, and Serenity hoped Shane wouldn't be too mad. Walking inside the house, they saw Shane was laid out on the couch, sleeping, and Serenity walked over to him, shaking him gently.

"Damn, what time is it?" Shane asked sleepily.

"It's two forty-five. If you want, you can go up in the guest room and sleep there for the night," Serenity suggested.

"Bitch, hell nah! I'm going home to sleep in the bed with my man. Them days of me sleeping in yo guest room came to an end when I got in house dick."

"Well, excuse me. I was only trying to help because I stayed out so late. Get yo funky ass on then," Serenity joked.

"And will! I'll talk to you tomorrow." Shane slipped into his boots and put on his coat before walking out the door.

Serenity and Reason both took a seat on the couch, turning on the TV.

"I know we probably shouldn't, but would you like another drink?" Serenity asked.

"I'm down with it if you are."

Serenity stood up and walked out the living room. She returned a few moments later with a bottle of tequila and two shot glasses. She opened the bottle, pouring the shots before handing one to Reason.

"What are we toasting to?" Reason asked, looking over at Serenity.

"To us. We toasting to us. To everything we want to be. To making both of our wildest dreams come true." They both raised their glasses, clinking them together, before downing the shot.

Serenity smiled at Reason as she looked into his eyes. She would have never thought from the day he first wheeled himself into her office that she would fall in love with the man he was. After her daughter's father, she never thought she would love anyone else. Yet there she was, back in love. This time, she just prayed it was for the long haul. They spent the rest of the night on the couch talking and taking shots until they fell asleep cuddled up right where they sat.

Reason woke up a few hours later with the sun beaming into his eyes. He gently tapped Serenity, waking her from her sound sleep, to let her know he was going home.

"You coming back?" Serenity asked, not ready for him to leave yet.

"Yeah, I'll be back. You wanna do something today?"

"Yeah, lay here and watch movies with you. Maybe order some Chinese food. I'm still a bit hungover from last night, so I wouldn't mind being lazy today," Serenity suggested.

"That sounds good to me. Let me just go home and change my clothes, then I'll be right back."

"You know, it would be easier if you just packed some stuff to keep here. Then, on days like today, you wouldn't have to go home just to change clothes."

"Oh, so I can get a drawer in yo dresser? Is that what you saying?" Reason asked.

"Yeah. Shit, you can get more than that if you want it."

"Shit, let me find out you wanna be mine forever." Reason smiled, kissing Serenity on her forehead before walking out the door.

<hr>

Reason pulled up to his home about twenty minutes later and noticed a black Range Rover parked in his driveway. Not knowing who was in the car, Reason grabbed his gun from his center console and hopped out the car. Thankfully, before he could make another move, the car window rolled down, and he saw Ace sitting in the driver's seat.

"Damn, yo ass was gon' shoot a nigga?" Ace laughed.

"Hell yeah, I ain't know who you was sitting here in my fuckin' driveway. You could have been some nigga tryin' to off me."

"I was just 'bout to leave when you pulled up. I was coming to check on you. I ain't talked to you in a minute and wanted to know how you were doing."

"I'm good, had a long night last night. I'm just coming here to get a change of clothes before I head back out."

"Word? What you get into last night?" Ace opened his door and got out his car, walking over to Reason.

"I got a new lil baby. In fact, I'ma go back over to her house soon. What brings you by though? I ain't seen or heard from you since the funeral."

"Yeah, I know. I was just trying to give you some space. I know you had a lot of healing to do, and I wanted you to do that. I know shit be hard after you lose your moms, trust me. I just wanted you to know that I been handling the business, and everything been straight." Ace needed to see where Reason's head was. He knew he hadn't made any drops or pickups, and Ace hoped he didn't want any parts of the business.

"Yeah, that's cool and all, but I'm 'bout to get back on my shit. I was gonna start making calls sometime next week, letting niggas know I was back and running shit. With my mama gone, it's only right that I keep the business going."

Those were not the words that Ace wanted to hear. He'd already told everyone that he was running shit and that they should all answer to him now. With Reason wanting to get back in the game, that would surely push him back down to second place. That was something Ace couldn't have, so he knew he would have to do something to ensure that didn't happen.

"You sure you ready to come back so soon?" Ace asked.

"Yeah, I'm good. It's time to get back to work."

Ace nodded his head. They stood outside, talking, for a few more moments before Ace got back into his car and pulled out the driveway. Reason walked inside his home, going straight to his bathroom to shower. Once he was dressed, he grabbed a small suitcase from his closet and dresser. He was excited about the fact that Serenity wanted him to leave clothes at her house. To him, it meant she was serious about their relationship, and there was nothing that Reason wanted more than Serenity. So, once he was packed, he made his way back to her house.

Chapter Fourteen

Ace arrived back to his home a few hours later, walking inside and laying his keys on the end table in the living room. Kalahni sat on their cream sectional, watching a movie. Ace smiled as he looked at her, happy to be coming home to his family. He took his seat next to her, rubbing her stomach before kissing her cheek.

"Where Easton at?" Ace asked.

"He upstairs sleeping. You know his bedtime is eight o'clock. I need my free time after spending all day with him. I love him to life, but he is a handful, especially now that I'm pregnant. It seem like I'm always tired now."

"I get it. Once you have my baby girl, we can wait a while before having any more children."

"Boy, after I have our daughter, we don't need no more kids. We have a boy and a girl. That's the perfect family."

"Yeah, we ah see 'bout that. I'm tryna nut in that pussy every chance I get."

"Boy, shut up." Kalahni laughed, playfully hitting Ace on his arm.

Kalahni had been on cloud nine ever since she'd left Reason. Ace was now giving her the life she thought she deserved. They lived in a huge six-bedroom five-bathroom home with a pool in the back. They were planning a massive wedding that was set for the following year. Ace let Kalahni know she didn't have a budget for her special day and encouraged her to get everything she wanted. Kalahni thought she was living like a queen, not giving a damn about the pain she'd caused anyone else.

"I went to see Reason today," Ace informed.

Kalahni looked over at him, stunned. She thought Reason was out the picture completely. There was never a second thought in her mind that he would ever be seen again. Now that Ace was bringing him up, she hoped it wouldn't come with problems.

"What made you go see him? What would be the point of that? That man is supposed to be out of our lives. Why would you meet up with him?" she asked, turning to face him, so they could be eye to eye.

"I needed to check his temperature, and I'm glad I did because now I know that nigga tryin' to get back in the game. He want to take back over his mama business, and you know I can't have that. That shit is mine, and I plan to keep it that way."

"What you gon' do?"

"Shit, I'ma handle that shit the way you know I'ma handle that shit. That nigga just gotta go."

Kalahni nodded her head, already knowing what he meant by that. She wanted to keep the money flowing in by any means, so she was down with whatever Ace wanted to do to make that happen.

"Do what you gotta do, baby. The quicker the better."

"I'm on it. This empire is ours, and I'm not gon' let nobody stand in the way of that. It's our time to shine, baby."

Kalahni knew that she could trust Ace to stay on top of everything. It was clear to her that Reason was oblivious to everything going on. If he wasn't, he would have made it be known when Ace saw him. Kalahni was happy the ball was still in their court. Knowing Ace would handle it, she let it go, curling up under him while they watched the movie together.

Several moments later, her phone was chiming, alerting her of a text. She was too comfortable underneath her man to even move. They watched one more movie before they made their way up to their room for the night.

The next morning when Kalahni got up, Ace was already gone, and she knew what he was going to do. She didn't feel an ounce of remorse because she knew it was something that had to happen. Getting out of bed, she went downstairs to cook breakfast for Easton. She knew he would be up at any minute and would be telling her he was hungry. Unlocking her phone to start her playlist, she saw the missed text she had from Tori.

> Hey, girl. I was just wondering f you wanted to do brunch.

Kalahni hadn't spoken with Tori since the day she left her sitting at a restaurant alone. There had been no explanation or conversation after, and Kalahni wanted to know what was going on. It was too late for brunch seeing how she didn't have a babysitter for Easton. However, she shot a quick text back to her, letting her know she could just come to her house, and she would cook. Her phone chimed a few seconds later with a reply.

> Cool, I can do that. Just send me the address.

Kalahni replied, not giving it a second thought as she sent her address to Tori. She knew no one was to know where she and Ace laid their heads; however, Tori was her girl. She knew Tori was good people and wouldn't allow any harm to come to her. Tori let her know she would be there by noon, and Kalahni continued to cook breakfast.

Easton came walking down the stairs about fifteen minutes later, and Kalahni was just cutting the last piece of fruit to put on his plate.

"Good morning, Mommy's big man. How did you sleep?"

"Good. After I eat breakfast, can I play my game?" Easton asked, walking over to his kids' table before taking his seat.

"Sure. But you have to make sure you eat all your food. I'm going to go take a shower because Auntie Tori is coming over. But after you finish eating, you can turn it on."

"Okay, Mommy. I promise I'm gon' eat every bite."

"Okay, baby. I'll be back down when I get out the shower."

Kalahni headed up to her en-suite bathroom and showered before putting on a long-sleeved, pink, cotton, two-piece set. She brushed her hair into a low ponytail before brushing her freshly done lashes. She applied lip gloss to her lips, slid into her pink Dior slides, and sprayed herself with Prada Candy. Kalahni smiled as she looked in the mirror and rubbed her stomach. Once she was done, she placed a pair of gold hoops in her ears with a matching necklace, and her look was complete.

Looking over at her clock, she saw it was eleven. With Tori going to be there within the hour, she decided to order the food they would eat on Door Dash. Since Starters was one of their favorite spots, she decided to order from there. Once she had everything ordered, Kalahni made her way downstairs. Easton was sitting on the couch, playing his game, and Kalahni took a seat next to him as she waited for her food to arrive.

About thirty minutes later, she was getting an alert, letting her know that her food had arrived. Once she'd placed it on the counter, she began taking the items out of the plastic containers before placing them on glass serving plates. She'd just gotten done throwing the containers away when her phone chimed. Looking over at it, she saw it was a text message from Tori.

> Hey, girl. Something came up. I'm sorry. But
> we can make arrangements for another time.
> I'll call you later tonight, so we can set it up.

Kalahni looked around at all the food she'd gotten and just shook her head. *Well, I guess I can warm the rest up for dinner,* she thought as she placed a few items on a plate for herself. She sat on the couch for the rest of the day, watching her son play his PlayStation.

Reason woke up to the light shining in his eyes. He rolled over, wrapping his arm around Serenity, pulling her closer to him. This was the first night he'd spent the night at her house without leaving before her daughter woke up. What was supposed to be them spending some late-night adult time had turned into them planning a family day. Reason was excited because he loved spending time with Serenity and Scotland. He planned to be in Serenity's life for the long run and wanted her to know that he would be there for Scotland as well.

"You want me to cook some breakfast?" Serenity asked.

"How 'bout we go out to breakfast? I can go back home and get dressed and be back to get y'all in about an hour."

"You brought clothes over here. Why do you have to go home and get dressed?"

"I brought some stuff but nothing to wear out to breakfast. You know we all gotta look good as a unit when we go out. It ain't gon' take me long. I'll be back in an hour, and we can go to breakfast before doing whatever else you and Scotland want to do. Sound good?"

"Yeah, that sounds good to me. I can get us dressed, and we'll be ready by the time you get back."

"Cool, let me go get dressed. I'll be right back." Reason kissed Serenity before making his way to his car.

Reason pulled into his driveway about twenty minutes later, going directly inside and up to his room. He didn't know what they would be doing today, but since they would have Scotland with them, he knew it would be something kid friendly. So, with that, he took a black Off White sweatsuit from his closet before getting into the shower.

Once he was out the shower and dressed, he realized he only had ten minutes to make it back to Serenity's house if he was going to be on time. He rushed out his door and pulled off down the street. He arrived back to Serenity's house fifteen minutes later and rang her doorbell. Both her and Scotland were ready to go as soon as he walked inside.

"She's hungry. I had to give her a banana to hold her over." Serenity laughed.

"Then let's go get lil mama some food." Reason walked over to Scotland and sat on the couch next to her. "I'm sorry I kept you waiting. You like pancakes, right?"

"Yeah, I love pancakes. But they got to have chocolate chips and whipped cream on the top," Scotland replied.

"Cool, I got a little card in my wallet that can get you all the pancakes you want with extra chocolate chips and whipped cream." Reason tapped his hand on his pocket, only to realize his wallet wasn't inside. He shook his head, knowing he'd left it in his pants packet at home.

"I gotta go back home and get my wallet. I left it in the pants I took off."

"It's cool. I can pay for the food. It's no big deal," Serenity replied, grabbing her purse.

"No, you won't. You not going in your purse for nothing. We can just go pick it up and go to a restaurant that's closer to my house. It will only take a minute for me to run in and get it."

Serenity nodded her head, and they all walked out the door. Serenity opened her garage, taking Scotland's booster seat from her car and placing it into the backseat of Reason's SUV. Once they were all inside, they took off, ready to start their first Sunday fun day. When they pulled up at Reason's house, there was a black Range Rover in the driveway.

"Man, what he want now? I done seen him more in the last two days than I have in the past two months," Reason spoke aloud.

"Who is that?" Serenity asked.

"My homeboy. Let me see what this nigga want. Y'all want to get out and come in? This should only take a minute, but I don't want y'all just sitting out here."

Serenity nodded her head before opening her door and getting out the car. She got Scotland from the backseat as she watched Reason walk up to the Range Rover.

"Mommy, I thought we were going to get pancakes?" Scotland asked as she looked up at Reason's house.

"We are. We just had to make a quick stop."

Serenity took Scotland by the hand and walked over to where Reason was standing just as Ace was getting out the car. Reason went to introduce them, but the moment she looked into Ace's face, her entire body froze. She was visibly frightened, and Reason turned to her.

"Baby, are you okay?" Reason asked, wrapping his arms around her. Ace still stood there with his hand held out as he waited for Serenity to shake it.

"I-I... we need to go." Serenity and Scotland began walking back toward Reason's car. Reason could see Serenity shaking as she walked away, and he couldn't understand what happened.

"Look, bro, you look busy. How 'bout I come back tomorrow morning? We need to talk out our business plans," Ace suggested.

"Yeah, that would be cool. Just call me before you come, so I can make sure I'm home."

"Cool." They dapped each other up before Ace got back into his SUV and pulled out of Reason's driveway.

Reason, not knowing what was going on, walked back to his car and got into the driver's seat. "Baby, you don't want to go to breakfast anymore? Lil mama wants some pancakes with chocolate chips and whipped cream. We gotta get those for her."

"Who was that man?" Serenity asked, looking over at Reason.

"That's my homeboy. He like my best friend. We've known each other since we were kids."

"Take me and my daughter home right now. I don't know what the fuck y'all got going on, but you will not involve my daughter in that shit."

Reason looked over at Serenity, confused. The look on her face was fear that Reason had never seen before. There were tears in her eyes, and her hands were still shaking. "Baby, I don't know what's going on. If you don't want to go out to eat anymore, that's fine. We can go inside and order from Door Dash. But you not gonna just leave without telling me what is wrong with you."

Serenity looked into his eyes, and she saw genuine concern. *Maybe he really doesn't know*, she thought to herself before agreeing to go inside to talk. She wanted to tell Reason what was going on but didn't want Scotland to overhear anything. Getting back out the car, they all walked to Reason's front door before entering the house.

"Mommy, I thought we were going to get pancakes? I'm hungry," Scotland whined the moment they walked into the house.

"I'm going to order you some pancakes right now," Reason spoke, pulling out his phone and opening the Door Dash app. "You wanna watch *My Little Pony* while you wait on your food?"

"Yayyyy. I love *My Little Pony*. Can I watch it while I eat my pancakes too?"

"You sure can. You can have whatever you want."

Serenity didn't say a word, mainly because she didn't know what to say. Reason had come into her life and brought her smile back. She could only hope he wasn't trying to play her. She was so confused that she didn't know what to believe. *Was this all a lie? Has he been playing me this entire time?*

"Are you ready to go talk?" Reason asked once he pressed play on the first episode of *My Little Pony.*

Serenity nodded her head, and Reason took her hand, taking her upstairs, so they could talk alone.

"What's wrong with you? We were supposed to be having a good day today. I don't understand what happened in the short time it took to get from your house to mine. Just tell me so I make it better. Whatever it is don't have to ruin our family fun day."

"Reason, that man that was just here, he was the man who killed Scotland's father," Serenity revealed.

"What?" Reason asked, perplexed. "Are you sure?"

"I told you I would never forget the man's face that killed him. He shot him right in front of me, and he died in my arms. I've never been so sure about something in my life." Tears began falling down her cheeks.

Reason rushed over to her, taking her into his arms and holding her tightly. He didn't know what was going on; however, he was going to make it his business to find out. He'd never seen Serenity cry, and the fact that she was doing so now broke his heart. She was so adamant that Ace was the one that killed her child's father that Reason knew it had to be true; he just didn't know why.

"What is Scotland's father's name?"

"Brice, but he was known in the hood as Woo," Serenity revealed.

The name didn't sound familiar to Reason, so he didn't have the answers she needed, but he would for damn sure get them — even if that meant getting them in blood. He loved Serenity and only wanted to see her smile. So, the fact that another man was causing tears to fall from her eyes made his blood boil.

"I don't know Woo, nor have I heard of him, but I don't like to see you like this. I promise you this is something that I will handle. Nobody is going to make you cry, and I don't go see about them. Not even me. Matter fact, I can find out what's up right now."

"Reason, I don't need you getting hurt. I can't lose another man I love. I know that's yo homeboy, but he is dangerous. I watched him gun down Woo like it was nothing. I can't have the same thing happen to you. That man is clearly dangerous."

"Baby, nothing is going to happen to me. And if it does, it won't be by his hands. There is no way I'm going to watch you cry and not do nothing about it. Any nigga that makes tears fall from yo eyes is a dead man. I want you to always know that I got you and I don't play about you."

"I love you, Reason, and I need you to be good. If you didn't know Woo, then it means it ain't got nothing to do with you. I don't need you to be getting hurt over something that ain't have shit to do with you."

"If it got something to so with you, then it's my business. This shit clearly hurt you, so I gotta handle this shit."

"Okay, Reason," Serenity said in defeat.

Reason kissed Serenity once more before they walked back down the stairs together. They joined Scotland in the living room while they waited on her food. They were both hungry as well, so Reason placed an order for them. They all decided to go skating once they were done eating because they still had promised Scotland that they would do something fun.

Moments later, the doorbell rang, and Reason walked over to the door, thinking he would be coming back with Scotland's food. However, when he opened the door, he was surprised to see Tori standing on the other side. She was the last person he would have expected to see at his door.

"Kalahni don't live here no more. We broke up," Reason spoke, thinking that was the reason for her visit.

"I know. I'm here to see you."

"Well, I'm sorry, but I'm busy right now." Reason attempted to close the door, but Tori placed her hand up, stopping him.

"Reason, please, this is very important. The information I have is something you're going to want to hear. It's about your mother and Easton." She knew the mention of those two names would get Reason's attention, and that was exactly what it did. Opening the door for her, she walked inside.

Serenity walked over to the door just as Tori was entering. Reason, seeing the look on Serenity's face, quickly introduced them to one another before letting Serenity know Tori had important information for him. Nodding her head, Serenity walked back into the living room while Reason took Tori downstairs to his office.

"What do you need to talk to me about, Tori?"

"Have you spoken with Ace?"

"Yeah, he was just here. But you told me that you had something to tell me about my mama and Easton. What does Ace have to do with either of them?"

"Everything. Reason, Ace is the reason neither one of them are here anymore."

Reason raised his eyebrow in confusion, not understanding what Tori was telling him. "What do you mean?"

Tori took a deep breath before answering. "Ace is Easton's father. He and Kalahni are getting married, and she's pregnant again."

Reason recoiled. There was no way Ace was Easton's father. Ace was his best friend, and Reason knew fucking with Kalahni was something he would never do. *What the fuck is this bitch on? She gotta be crazy if she thinks I'm gone believe that shit.*

"Ace is Easton's father? Who told you that?"

"Kalahni did. Shit, Ace did too. Well, Ace confirmed that him and Kalahni was getting married. But she told me he was Easton's father."

Reason took a seat at his desk. Out of all the things Tori could have told him, he would have never thought this would be one of them. *Ace is supposed to be my muthafuckin' brother, yet he watched me raise a baby he knew wasn't mine? Now he bout to marry my old bitch? This nigga.* Reason couldn't believe what he was hearing.

"What about my mama? You said you had some information about her?"

"Ace killed her, Reason. Now that he told me out his own mouth. They were fucking. Ace was trying to get her to hand him her organization, so he thought he could get it by fucking her. She found out he was fucking Kalahni. I'm not sure how she found out, but she did. When she confronted him and told him she was going to tell you, he killed her."

Rage built up inside of Reason, and he wished he could put hands on Ace right then. He couldn't believe this was happening. Ace was his right-hand and had been by his side through everything, all the while being a snake.

"Why are you just now telling me this?"

Tori lowered her head. Although she knew he would ask, this was the question she'd been dreading. There was no need to start hiding now. She was exposing the truth, so she might as well tell the entire truth out.

"I was fucking Ace too. I thought we were going to be together. I knew he was fucking yo mama, but he promised me it was only so he could get us straight. Then, I found out he was marrying Kalahni, and everything changed. Ace is not a good person. And on top of all that, he tried to kill you too."

"Get y'all straight?"

"Yeah, he promised me that once Peaches gave him the business then I wouldn't want for anything. He promised me that we would be good, but that was all a lie."

"What do you mean he tried to kill me?"

"You being paralyzed was no accident. He wanted you to be dead. He paid someone to hit y'all that night. That's why he drove, and the car was hit on the side you were on," Tori lied. The truth was that she'd been the one to set up the accident. She didn't know why she added that lie seeing how the truth was enough for Reason to body Ace; however, she did.

Reason took in everything Tori told him, already knowing what he had to do. If seeing Serenity cry wasn't reason enough to kill him, finding out what he'd done to Peaches was. He would have never thought Ace would have done any of this and couldn't understand how it had been done right under his nose.

"I got the address where they are staying if you want it," Tori informed.

"Yeah, let me get that."

Tori wrote down the address on a piece of paper before handing it over to Reason. She was smiling inside, knowing that all her problems were about to come to an end. Reason walked Tori to the door before walking back into the living room to see Serenity sitting there with Scotland. Her pancakes had finally arrived, and she was enjoying them while she watched her cartoons.

"I gotta go. Y'all can stay here, or I can drop you off at home."

Serenity could see the change in his demeanor and wanted to know why. Getting up from the couch, she walked over to him.

"What happened? I thought we were going skating."

"We were, but something came up."

Serenity looked into his eyes and saw the anger in them. His eyes were cold, and she didn't recognize the man that looked back at her.

"Baby, what happened? Is this about Ace?"

When Reason didn't answer, she knew she was spot on. Taking his hand, she walked him out the living room and out of Scotland's earshot. She didn't want anything to happen to Reason. So, she knew she needed to stop him before it did. She'd never seen him so mad, and it scared her. Serenity had gone through the loss of a love once, and it almost killed her. She couldn't go through it again because she feared this time, she wouldn't be as strong.

"Are you staying here or going home?"

Reason didn't have time for anything else. He was going to handle his business and nothing Serenity or anyone else said was going to stop him. Ace had killed his mother, and behind that, he had to die.

"I'm staying here, but I wish you would just listen to me."

"I'm going to be out late. If Scotland wants to go to sleep, she can sleep in Easton's old room. His bed is still in there, and there are new sheets and covers in the hall closet."

"I wish you would just take a minute and listen to me. I don't know what you plan to do, but I wish you would just listen to me please, Reason."

Without saying another word, Reason walked up the stairs, heading to his room. Serenity was on his heals, not letting up. Her heart raced with every step she took. She'd never knew this side of Reason, and she felt that in the state he was in, he would do something he would regret later.

Reason walked to his room, going directly to his closet. He pulled out a black hoodie, a pair of black sweatpants, and a pair of black leather gloves. He then pulled out a black duffle bag that he set on the bed before placing a change of clothes inside. Reason then slid his hands into the leather gloves, making sure they were secure. There would be no fingerprints left on anything he touched, so he knew he would be keeping the gloves on until he returned home. The sight of the gloves made Serenity's eyes widen as she continued to plead with Reason not to go. However, her pleas fell on deaf ears.

Walking back into his closet, Reason opened one of his closet drawers and pulled out two .9mm pistols. He placed a silencer onto one of the guns before placing it inside the duffle bag. He then tucked the other into his waistline. Serenity looked on in horror, already knowing what Reason was going to do.

"Reason, please. He's not worth it," Serenity pleaded one last time.

"He killed my mother. It's nothing you can say that's going to stop me from going. I promise you I'm going to be fine. Ain't shit gon' happen to me. I'll be back as soon as I can. If you end up wanting to leave, there is a spare key in the kitchen drawer. Just make sure you lock the door." Reason kissed Serenity's forehead before walking out the door.

Serenity's heart dropped when she heard the door close behind him. She dropped to her knees that moment, praying to God that nothing would happen to Reason. Serenity loved Reason, and even though he didn't know it, Reason had healed her heart the same way she'd healed his, allowing her to love and be happy again, and that was something she didn't want to lose.

Standing back to her feet, she placed a fake smile on her face as she walked back downstairs, joining her daughter in the living room.

"Mommy, are we still going skating?" Scotland asked, not taking her eyes off the TV.

"Not today. Reason got called into work," she lied. "But he told us we can stay here til he gets back. We can order all the food and snacks you want and watch all the cartoons you want. And I promise, next weekend, we gonna go skating and to the movies."

"Yayyy! Okay, we can stay here. Reason's house is really big, Mommy. Can we play hide and seek? I bet that would be fun in this big ol' house."

"Sure, baby, we can do whatever you want. I think hide and seek will be fun too," Serenity replied before she began counting. They played hide and seek before ordering snacks from Door Dash and watching cartoons.

Chapter Fifteen

Reason pulled the folded piece of paper that Tori had given him from his pocket and put the address into his GPS. Seeing the address was an hour and a half away, he pulled out his driveway, heading to his destination. His trigger finger itched as he gripped the steering wheel. Murder was the only thing that was on his mind, and he knew the moment he saw Ace, there would be no talking. He thought about the way things had played out leading up to the death of his mother.

"That nigga was asking about her organization a lot. Now I know why," Reason spoke aloud. "And he was fuckin' my mama and my bitch. This nigga had me raising his son while he sat back and watched. Kinda pussy ass shit is that? I'm going to kill this bitch ass nigga with my bare hands."

Reason hit his steering wheel in frustration as he realized the person that was supposed to be his best friend was the cause of all his pain. He couldn't understand why he'd done this to him, and at that point, he didn't give a fuck. What was done had already been done; now Reason would have to handle things the only way he saw fit. His mother didn't deserve what Ace handed to her, so Reason was going to make sure Ace felt every bit of the pain he did. His mother would be proud of the things he would do to Ace, and Reason was going to make sure of it.

Exactly an hour and a half later, Reason was pulling down Ace's street. He looked at the huge houses on the street as he drove slowly. He stopped across the street when he saw he'd made it to his destination. He sat there in his car, looking at the massive brick home. It was the middle of the afternoon, and although he wanted to bust in and shoot up everything, he knew he would have to be smart about it.

He set in the car for several moments, just looking over at the house, until the door opened. He watched as Easton and Kalahni walked outside. His heart dropped once he saw Easton's little face. This was the first time he'd seen him since the funeral, and he wanted to run to him, kiss his little cheeks, and tell him how much he missed him. However, he knew he couldn't. Easton was not his, and no matter how much it hurt, that was something he would have to live with. For a split second, his heart began to warm as he watched Easton be put into the backseat of Kalahni's G-wagon.

The moment they pulled out the driveway, Reason got out the car, jogging across the street and around to the back of the house. Finding an open window, he used one of the lawn chairs that set by the pool to stand up on while he climbed through the window. He walked around the home, looking at the pictures on the wall. He noticed the family picture they'd taken together. They were in matching all white fits, and Ace held Easton in his arms as he placed his other hand onto Kalahni's stomach. Reason couldn't believe how his right-hand had come in and stole his family away from him.

Taking his gun out of his waistline, he walked through the house, looking into every room, making sure nobody else was there. Reason had just made his way downstairs when he heard someone coming to the door. He smiled, knowing that he was about to get revenge for his mother. Walking slowly toward the front door with his gun leading the way, he came face-to-face with Ace.

"What the fuck? Reason, you scared me." Ace jumped. It hadn't yet dawned on him that Reason was standing in his home — the one he shared with Kalahni and the one no one should have the address to.

Reason chuckled, cocking his gun and aiming it directly at Ace. Reason hadn't come to play, and he wanted Ace to know that. Just the sight of him made Reason want to empty his clip.

"You didn't expect to see me here, huh? Just like I bet my mama didn't think that you would be the one that killed her, right?"

Ace's eyes widened at the mention of Peaches' murder. He knew exactly who had told Reason that information. Tori was the only person he had told that he'd killed Peaches, so he knew if Reason knew, it was only because she told him. Ace could have kicked himself. It was Tori's hurt feelings that caused her to turn against him, and he knew that. At that moment, he wished he could turn back the hands of time. Yet there he was, staring down the barrel of Reason's gun. Ace knew it was over for him. All the dirt he did had finally caught up to him, and there was no one to get him out of it.

"Where is Kalahni and Easton?" Ace asked, looking Reason directly in his eyes. Now wasn't the time for fear. What was done was done, and he'd been caught unarmed.

"They left before I came in. I ain't gon' kill you in front of them. But they definitely gon' be the ones to find yo body. I just got one question. Why did you do it?"

"You had the perfect life, and I wanted it," Ace revealed, standing tall on his words and not giving a damn how fucked up they sounded.

With that, there was nothing left to say. Reason pulled his trigger, firing shots into Ace until he had no more bullets left. Putting his gun back into his waistline, Reason placed his hood over his head before exiting Ace's home.

***

Reason walked back into his home several hours later. Serenity and Scotland were sitting on his couch watching TV. He spoke before heading directly upstairs to his en-suite bathroom. Opening the cupboard underneath his sink, Reason pulled out a large brown paper bag. He placed his clothes and shoes inside before getting into the shower. He scrubbed every inch of his body, rinsing off in hot water before scrubbing again. Reason remained in the shower for forty-five minutes.

"Reason, what happened?" Serenity asked, walking into the bathroom as he showered.

"Shit, it went the way I knew it would. He killed my mother, so you shouldn't have to ask what happened. Can we talk about this when I get out the shower?"

"Sure," Serenity answered as she walked out the bathroom, heading back down the stairs.

Once out the shower, Reason put on a pair of gray sweatpants, a white t-shirt, and a pair of Nike slides before grabbing the paper bag and going into his backyard. He placed the bag into his barbeque grill and set it on fire, being sure everything turned to ash before putting out the fire and closing his grill.

Serenity came outside a few moments later, letting Reason know Scotland was taking a nap on the couch. Reason knew she wanted to talk, so he grabbed her hand and led her up to his bedroom. They both sat on his bed, and Serenity looked into his eyes.

"Reason, please tell me you didn't kill that man."

"I can't tell you that and be telling the truth. You want me to lie?"

Serenity's heart sank. As happy as she was that Reason had come back home, she knew the type of trouble killing someone could bring.

"Reason, what if you go to prison? What then?"

"I'm not going to no damn prison," he answered.

Serenity scoffed, looking into his eyes, perplexed. "How are you so sure? You act like this is a regular thing for you."

Reason didn't say a word, just looked at her. His silence told it all, and she opened her mouth to speak again. "You told me you were in real estate. I don't know a real estate agent that's this comfortable with killing someone."

Reason lowered his head. He'd forgotten what he'd told Serenity he did for a living. He felt bad for lying to her, so he figured this was the perfect time to tell the truth. Grabbing her hand, he looked into her eyes.

"You're not in real estate, are you?"

"No. Serenity, I'm not. The truth is my mother ran the top drug organization in Michigan. And now, the organization belongs to me. I'm sorry I lied, but that's not something you just tell people, ya know? I completely understand if you don't want to fuck with me anymore. I know the life I live is not for everyone."

Serenity didn't speak. Instead, she leaned into him, placing her hand onto his face before kissing his lips softly. She saw the pain of loss and betrayal in his eyes, and that broke her heart. Placing her forehead against his, she gently rubbed the back of his neck. The feelings Serenity had for Reason were strong. He was her second chance at love, and there was no way she could just let that go.

"I'm never leaving you, Reason. You've shown me something about myself that I didn't know. You showed me I could love again, and that's something I never thought would be possible. Loving you makes me so happy, and that's something I don't want to lose."

With those words, Serenity saw all the pain in his eyes leave, and all she saw was love. She saw the man she knew she could spend the rest of her life with. He kissed her lips passionately for several moments before breaking their embrace. He looked deeply into her eyes, and she smiled back at him.

"I love you, Serenity."

"I love you too. Just don't lie to me again. You never have to hide or lie about who you are to me. I should be the one person that you're able to be yourself with."

"I promise it will never happen again, baby. I want us to be forever."

Chapter Sixteen

Tori lay in bed, smoking a blunt, as she thought about today's events. She knew she'd done her big one today, and she couldn't wait to hear about the outcome. Looking over at her clock, Tori saw that it was after three in the morning. She smiled, knowing that by now, Ace was dead. She took a deep pull from the blunt, blowing the smoke through her lips before removing the covers from her body and getting out of her bed. Walking down to her kitchen, Tori poured herself a glass of wine, wanting to celebrate her success with a drink.

Heading back up to her room, she grabbed her laptop and took a seat at her desk. Feeling good about the move she'd made, she felt as though she deserved to get herself something nice. *I'm going onto the Gucci website.* She scrolled through the items before finding herself several that she wanted to purchase. Once she had everything ordered, she decided to get some sleep, hoping that she would have news on Ace when she woke up.

She felt as though she had only been sleeping for a few minutes when her phone rang. Jumping up from her sleep, she grabbed her phone, looking down at the screen to see it was Kalahni. She swiped the talk button and answered the phone, already knowing the reason for the call.

"Toriiiii, he's gone! He's gone, Tori. I don't know what to do.

Easton walked in first and found him. The police been at my house for hours and literally just left. Lord, Tori, what do I do?"

"Kalahni, calm down. I don't understand what you're saying to me. Who's gone?"

"Ace! He's dead, Tori. When me and Easton came home, he was laying on the floor all shot up. Tori, he's gone, and I don't know what to do. Easton won't stop crying. He keeps having nightmares every time he closes his eyes. I just don't know what to do," Kalahni cried into the phone.

Tori smiled, loving every minute of the pain Kalahni felt. Kalahni didn't know anything about Tori and Ace having a relationship; however, in Tori's mind, she was the reason they couldn't be together. For that, she felt that Kalahni needed to pay.

"He's dead? What do you mean? What happened?"

"I don't know. Someone must have come into the house and shot him. I don't know who, and I have no idea why. Nobody even knows where we live."

"Where are you now, Kalahni?" Tori asked. It was not because she cared about Kalahni's wellbeing, but she knew it was time to put the next part of her plan in motion.

"I just checked into a hotel. I can't stay in that house anymore after seeing my fiancé laid out on the floor like that. We had our entire life ahead of us, and now we ain't got shit. Ain't no life to look forward to because he's dead. My man is gone, Tori. I have a son who was just now getting to know Ace as his father and a daughter inside of me that will never know him at all. This is too much." Kalahni's breaths became fast as she began to hyperventilate. She felt as though she couldn't breathe as she thought about what her life would be like in the future.

"Calm down, Kalahni. I'm going to help you get through this. Send me the address of the hotel you're in, and I'll get dressed and drive to you."

"Thank you, Tori. I knew I could count on you."

Several moments later, Tori received a text with the hotel and room number where Kalahni was staying. Once she was dressed, she grabbed her keys and purse before heading to her car. Once she put the address in her GPS, she pulled out her driveway and made her way to Kalahni.

Tori pulled into the parking lot of the hotel about an hour and a half later. She parked before getting out of her car and walking inside the lobby of the luxurious hotel. *Damn, even in the midst of tragedy, this bitch gone still be in style.* Tori made her way to the elevators before taking it up to the twentieth floor. She found Kalahni's room and knocked on the door.

She knocked for several moments, and she didn't understand why it was taking Kalahni so long to come to the door. However, when the door finally opened, Tori couldn't believe her eyes. Kalahni stood on the other side, blood running from between her legs.

"I need to go to the hospital," Kalahni spoke as she looked over at Tori.

"Oh, my God! Start walking to the elevator. I'll get Easton and take you to the hospital."

Tori rushed into the room, waking a sleeping Easton, before placing his shoes onto his feet. She grabbed his coat before picking him up and running out the room. Tori truly tried to get Kalahni to the hospital as fast as she could, not wanting anything to happen to the baby she was carrying. However, it was too late. Kalahni lost the baby before they even made it to the hospital. Although Tori didn't want Kalahni to lose her baby, she thought the fact that she did was the rest of her karma for the part she played in her heartache.

Over the next several days, Tori stayed with Kalahni, helping her with Easton as much as she could. Tori deserved an Oscar for the role she was playing. Hell, she fooled herself as she played the role of the loving best friend. She knew Kalahni didn't suspect a thing, and that was how she planned to keep it until it was too late for her.

"I'm 'bout to go run a couple of errands. Do you want me to take Easton with me?" Tori asked as she walked into the room. Kalahni was lying in bed, the same as she had since she'd come back from the hospital.

"Yeah, thank you," Kalahni responded, not even lifting her head from her pillow. Kalahni felt like the beautiful life she'd planned had been ripped away from her, and she couldn't understand why things had played out the way they did. She thought her and Ace would have years of greatness together, but it was all cut short.

Once Tori helped Easton into his shoes and jacket, they left the hotel room. They took the hour and a half drive back to Tori's house.

Walking inside her home, she took Easton to her living room, turning on cartoons for him before walking into the kitchen to grab him a snack. It was time to finish out her plan, and today would be the day she did so.

Walking up to her room, Tori grabbed the plane ticket she'd purchased along with her passport and put them both into her purse. She packed her bag, only taking the things she would need to start over — her important papers, her jewelry, all of her bank cards, several outfits, and the money she'd been saving. Taking her gun from her nightstand drawer, she placed it into her purse before taking everything to her car.

Walking back into her house, she gathered Easton and headed back out to the hotel. Tori was more than ready for this to come to an end, and that was exactly what she was about to do. Pulling into the parking lot, Tori grabbed her purse and Easton before walking inside the hotel. When she walked into the room, Kalahni was still in the bed like Tori knew she would be. She sat Easton on the couch, grabbing his iPad and placing his headphones on his ears, before turning on a movie for him to watch.

Tori walked into the bathroom, pulling out her gun and placing the silencer onto it before walking back into the bedroom Kalahni was in, closing the door behind her.

"How you feeling?" Tori asked.

"Fucked up. I lost the love of my life and my daughter back to back. I feel like I want to die. Shit, if it wasn't for Easton being in the next room, I would be dead."

"Don't worry, you're gonna be."

"Huh?" Kalahni asked weakly, not understanding what Tori was saying to her.

"I just want to know how you thought you could get everything by hurting everyone around you, and shit was just gon' be sweet. Nah, bitch, it's yo time now."

With those words, Kalahni sat up in bed, looking over at Tori. When she saw the gun that was being pointed at her, her eyes widened in shock.

"Tori, what the hell is going on?" Kalahni asked frantically, holding her hands up in surrender.

"You thought you could just take my man, huh? You thought you was gon' live happily ever after with Ace, and I was just gon' let that happen? Nah, bitch, it's time for you to pay for that shit just like he had to."

"Where is my son?"

"Don't worry, Easton is safe. He in there watching movies. Don't worry 'bout him. It ain't like you gon' see him ever again anyway. Since you wanted to be with my man so fuckin' badly, you can join his ass in the afterlife."

"Why do you keep calling Ace yo man? Tori, just put the gun down, so we can talk about this. We better than this. We ain't letting no man come between us."

"Because he was my man before you came to me, telling me y'all was getting married. Bitch, you thought you was just gon' take him from me, and I was just gon' let y'all be happy? Well, ho, if I can't be happy with the nigga then nobody will."

"Tori, you killed Ace?"

"Nah, Reason did that part for me. I'm gon' kill you though. Be sure to tell Ace that I love him when you see him." With that, Tori fired three shots into Kalahni's chest before placing the gun into her waistline. Rushing out the door and closing it behind her, she grabbed Easton before walking out of the hotel room as calmly as she could. Putting Easton into the backseat of her car, she pulled out the parking lot, waiting until she was several miles away from the hotel before she took off the red wig she was wearing, throwing it out the window right before she merged onto the freeway.

"Tori, can we go to McDonald's? I'm hungry," Easton asked.

"Sure, we can go get you some McDonald's, then I'ma take you to see yo daddy."

"Mommy said my real daddy was Uncle Ace, and he not coming back. But I don't know how Uncle Ace is my daddy when my daddy is my daddy. So, are you taking me to see Uncle Ace or my daddy?" Easton was so confused, and his little mind couldn't understand all the betrayal his mother had put everyone around her through.

"I'm taking you to see your daddy. Reason is your daddy, Easton. He really loves you more than anybody in this world. And out of all the people around you, he's the only one that deserves to have you."

"Yayyy, I miss him so much. Mommy told me I wasn't ever gonna see him again. I'm sooo happy," Easton cheered.

Tori smiled, happy that some good had come out of all this after all. No, Easton would not have his mother anymore, but Tori felt the love that Reason had for Easton would be enough. *He better off without Kalahni. Lord knows the type of life he would have had to live with her raising him,* Tori thought to herself.

After getting the McDonald's that she'd promised Easton, Tori pulled over to a park, so they could eat. Although it was too cold for him to play, they watched an episode of *Spider-Man* on Easton's tablet as they eat. When they were done, Tori gathered all the empty containers, placing them into the McDonald's bag.

"I'll be right back," Tori informed, getting out the car and walking away.

She walked until she found a trash can. Using the McDonald's napkins that she'd brought with her; she took her gun from her waistline before wiping it clean. Once she was certain all of her fingerprints were off of it, she placed it into the McDonald's bag before placing the bag into the trash and making her way back to her car.

"You ready to go?" she asked, looking over at Easton.

"Yep." Easton crawled back into the backseat, and they made their way to Reason's house.

Tori pulled into the driveway, leaving her car running as she walked Easton up to Reason's front door. She rang the doorbell twice before running back to her car. The moment she saw the door open, she pulled out the driveway and took off up the street before anyone could stop her with any questions.

Getting back onto I-94, she went west toward the airport. She drove for several miles before thinking twice about boarding a flight. Tori wasn't sure if it was just paranoia or God telling her flat out not to do it. Either way, she was going to follow her first mind. Getting off at the next exit, Tori turned around, going back east as she headed toward the bridge to Canada. She was leaving the United States and everything in her past behind her as she went on to begin a new life in another country.

Chapter Seventeen

Reason opened his front door and was taken aback by what he saw. Standing there was the first little heart that Reason had ever loved. Reason stood there, shocked, not believing his eyes. He looked around, not seeing anyone else with him, before squatting down and giving Easton a hug.

"Daddy, I missed you so much. Mommy told me I wasn't gonna see you again."

"Where is your mommy, Easton?" Reason asked, not understanding how Easton had gotten on his porch.

"She's at the hotel, sleep. Tori brought me to see you," Easton revealed.

Reason closed the door behind him before walking Easton into the living room. Serenity and Scotland were sitting on the couch, and Serenity looked up at Reason as she watched him bring a little boy she'd never seen before into the room.

"Reason, baby, who is this?" Serenity asked, confused as she stood from the couch.

"I need to talk to you," Reason replied. "Easton, this is Scotland. How about the two of you sit here and watch cartoons and eat some cookies?" Reason suggested, looking down at Easton.

"Okay, Daddy."

Serenity looked up at Reason, confused, before following him out of the living room. They headed up the stairs before walking into the master bedroom.

"Reason, what's going on? Is that Easton, as in the little boy you thought was your son?"

"Yes, that's him. I have no idea what's going on. He said that his mom was in a hotel sleep, and Tori brought him here. I don't even know why. Kalahni can't know he's here because she told me I would never see him again."

"And this don't seem strange to you? What are the odds that he would just show up on your doorstep after all this time? And if that Tori girl did bring him, then where is she? Why would she just drop him off on the porch and pull off without even making sure he got into the house safely?"

"I don't know," Reason replied honestly.

"Do you have her number?"

"Tori's? Nah."

"You need to go see if Easton knows his mother's number. We don't need yo ass in the middle of no fucking Amber Alert."

Reason nodded his head, walking out the room and heading back down to Easton. He sat on the couch next to him before asking him if he had a way of calling Kalahni.

"Yeah, I can call her on my iPad." Easton went to his contacts before calling his mother on FaceTime. When she didn't answer, he called her once more. When she still didn't answer, Reason decided they would try again later. After helping Easton out of his shoes so that he could get comfortable on the couch, they watched movies for several hours before placing another call to Kalahni.

When she didn't answer this time, Reason began to worry. Not only was it unusual for Easton to be at his house, but the fact that Kalahni wasn't answering her phone for him just wasn't right. There was no way Kalahni just wasn't answering the phone for Easton. Reason knew something was wrong, and he was going to get to the bottom of it. That night, Easton slept in his old bed for the first time in months.

The next morning, Reason woke up and went right to Easton's room to wake him. When he wasn't inside his room, Reason instantly became panicked, not seeing Easton lying in bed. After calling his name as he looked around the room and not finding him, Reason rushed out the door. He ran down the stairs, calling Easton's name with each step.

"I'm right here, Daddy," Easton called out. He was sitting at the kitchen table, eating the breakfast that Serenity prepared.

"You good?" Serenity asked, looking at the way Reason rushed into the kitchen.

"Yeah, I just didn't know where he was. I thought... Never mind. How is everyone doing this morning?"

"Good. Mommy made pancakes with chocolate chips," Scotland informed.

"Sit down so I can make you a plate," Serenity suggested.

Reason nodded his head before taking his seat. Serenity placed his breakfast plate in front of him before she took a seat at the table herself. The four of them sat and ate breakfast together before Reason informed Serenity that he was going to place a call to Kalahni's mother. He knew it might be a long shot, but he hoped she would know where Kalahni was.

"Hello?" Michelle answered.

"Hey, it's Reason. I know it's been a minute, but I was wondering if you knew where Kalahni was or heard from her? Easton was left..."

"Before you finish that sentence, let me just tell you that I don't give a fuck. Easton is y'all child, and y'all need to take care of him y'all self. I raised my kids. I'm not 'bout to be raising my grandkids unless you tryna give up some money."

Reason rolled his eyes the moment Michelle mentioned money. He knew then that he would never take Easton to her. It was clear that Kalahni didn't communicate with her at all. *This bitch still thinks Easton is my son*, Reason thought for several more moments. *I signed his birth certificate; I'm listed on all of his medical records as his father. I could just be his father. Who would know?*

With that, Reason hung up the phone, placing a call to the police and reporting Kalahni missing. He didn't know exactly what was going on, but he knew if he was going to take over custody of Easton, he would have to cover his tracks. Reason was informed that he would need to come to the station to file an official report. Reason agreed, getting dressed before letting Serenity know he would be back as soon as he was done.

Reason walked into the police station about fifteen minutes later. Walking up to the desk, he let the officer know he was there to file a missing person's report.

"What's the name and relation of the person?" the officer asked.

"Kalahni Everheart and she's my son's mother."

"When was the last time you saw her?"

"I haven't seen or spoken with her in a few months. We broke up a while ago. Yesterday, my son was dropped off at my doorstep. My son said his mother was in a hotel room sleeping, but every time he tried calling her, there was no answer. It's not like her to just leave our son."

"Do you or your son know the name of the hotel she was staying in?"

"No, I don't. And my son just turned three, so he wasn't able to tell me anything either."

The officer nodded her head and typed in a few words into her computer. After gathering Reason's contact information, she let him know they would be in contact, and Reason walked out the station. He prayed that everything would be okay. If nothing else, Kalahni was Easton's mother, and he didn't want anything to happen to her for that reason alone.

When he arrived home, Serenity was walking out the door with both Scotland and Easton. Getting out of his car, he walked up to them.

"Where y'all off to?"

"They asked if I could take them to Chuck E Cheese, but Easton don't have any clothes, so we're going shopping before we go to Chuck E Cheese," Serenity responded.

Reason smiled before letting Serenity know he would go with them. If Reason hadn't been in love before, he knew at that moment he was genuinely in love with Serenity. Here she was, showing love to a child she didn't even know and treating him the way she would her own son.

They headed to Reason's Rover, making their way to the mall to buy both Easton and Scotland new outfits. Serenity took Easton into the dressing room of one of the stores, putting on one of the outfits they'd brought him. Reason had planned on Easton being with him for the long run, so he was sure to buy him enough clothes to last a few months.

After spending a couple hours in the mall, they were finally ready to go to Chuck E Cheese. They walked inside about twenty minutes later. They walked up to the register and bought a family bundle package. They knew how much the kids loved Chuck E Cheese, and they both wanted them to be able to play as long as they wanted to.

"Your kids are so cute," the cashier complimented.

"Thank you," Serenity smiled. taking the game cards from her before they all walked to their table.

They had a wonderful time together as a family, and for the first time in a long time, Reason felt complete. He wasn't sure how the tables had turned, and everything had worked out in his favor, but it was happy it did. There he was, sitting there with the love of his life, while he watched not one but their two children play together. Life was good, and Reason couldn't have been happier.

A week had passed, and there had been no word on Kalahni's whereabouts. Serenity and Scotland had been staying at Reason's house every night. Reason and Serenity had redecorated Easton's room, being sure to add every Spider-Man detail that he wanted. They'd even redecorated one of the guest rooms, making it a beautiful princess bedroom for Scotland. Although they hadn't moved in with Reason, he wanted Scotland to have her own comfortable space on the nights they stayed over.

It was a Thursday night, and Serenity had ordered pizza per Easton's request. She didn't really feel like cooking after the day she had at the office. So, when Easton asked for pizza, she jumped right on it. She'd just gotten out the shower and slipped into her pajamas when the doorbell chimed.

"Don't worry, baby. I'll go get the pizza," Reason offered, jogging down the stairs and heading to the front door. He was surprised when he opened it to find two officers standing on the other side.

"Good evening, Officers. How can I help you?"

"We are looking for Reason Alexander. Are you him?"

"Yes, what can I do for you?"

"Mr. Alexander, we are here because of the missing person's report you filed a week ago on a Kalahni Everhart. I'm sorry to inform you, Mr.

Alexander, but we have found a body that we believe to be hers. It was inside a hotel room in Lansing. We have a picture here for you to look at and see if you can give us a positive ID."

Reason nodded his head slowly, being caught off guard by the officer's discovery. Never in a million years would he have thought this would be the outcome, and he prayed that the woman on the picture was not Kalahni. His heart sank in his chest when he saw the picture and realized it was indeed Kalahni.

"I'm sorry for your loss, sir. We will indeed start a full criminal investigation, and we hope to find justice for your loved one."

Reason nodded his head and watched as the two officers walked away and headed back to their car.

Reason went right to the living room, grabbing his phone to call Michelle. Even though she was a horrible mother, Reason still felt that she had the right to know that her daughter had been murdered. To his surprise, she was genuinely hurt, crying into the phone as she asked the details. Reason told Michelle everything he knew while also giving her the number of the detective. He let her know that he would help with the funeral costs if she needed him to before he ended the call. That night, Reason was forced to inform Easton that his mother was never coming back.

Chapter Eighteen

It had been six months since Kalahni's funeral, and things were finally starting to get back to normal. Although Easton missed his mother and still asked about her every day, Serenity had become like a second mother to him. She agreed fully when Reason sat down with her and let her know he wanted Easton to stay with them. With Reason already being his father on paper, they never had to go through family court. Just like that, they were now a family of four.

Serenity walked into her kitchen, taking the last cardboard box from the counter and walking it outside to the U-Haul. It was moving day, and she couldn't have been happier. Serenity and Reason had bought a six-bedroom four-bathroom home in West Bloomfield together, and she couldn't wait to start their new life.

"Okay, babe, that's everything," Serenity informed.

"Then let's go home, baby."

They both got into the truck and made their way to their new home. The house was huge, and Serenity never thought she would live in a house so massive. While she lived comfortably in the three-bedroom home she bought when Scotland was first born, she welcomed the change. She smiled as Reason pulled into the driveway of the black and white home with floor to ceiling windows. The large home set on an acre of land, which had all been well-manicured, and she couldn't wait to plant flowers. There was also a large wooden deck in the back of the house with a Jacuzzi and a pool. The house seemed to be their own little oasis, and she couldn't wait to make the house a home.

Shane had volunteered to keep Scotland and Easton for the weekend while Reason and Serenity moved into the new home. She was grateful for that because she knew the moving process would have been twice as hard with them being there. Serenity walked up the walkway of her white stone home with black trim, walking onto the porch before entering the code into the keypad. She was just about to walk inside the home when Reason stopped her.

"Nah, you not walking over this threshold for the first time. I don't even get down like that. Come here, queen."

Reason picked Serenity up, carrying her through the door. Serenity giggled before laying her head on his shoulder. She was so happy and couldn't wait to spend the rest of her life with him. He walked her across the dark hardwood floors and up the stairs.

"Baby, where are we going? We have to get the rest of the boxes from the truck," Serenity asked, still giggling.

"I heard it was bad luck to bring in any boxes before at least christening one room of the house. We can't start our new life with bad luck."

"Boy, shut up." Serenity laughed.

Once up to their bedroom, Reason walked into their en-suite bathroom before placing her onto the counter. They kissed passionately before Reason began sliding her black leggings from her waist. She rose up from the counter a bit, so he could slide the leggings over her plump backside. Dropping to his knees, he placed his head between her legs and began feasting on her wetness. Serenity moaned loudly, grinding her hips onto his face. Reason grabbed her hips, pulling her closer to him, so he could go deeper into her wetness.

"Yes, Daddy, that's it. Just like that," Serenity moaned seductively as she grabbed his head.

When Serenity began creaming, Reason was sure to clean up ever drop before standing to his feet and pulling out his rock-hard manhood. Serenity wrapped her legs around his waist, pulling him into her as he entered her wetness. Her tightness caused him to moan with each stroke.

"This shit feels so good, baby. You gon' make me cum in this pussy."

"Cum in me, baby. Feed this pussy, Daddy," Serenity called out, causing Reason to do just that. They kissed each other, allowing their tongues to dance.

Reason released his seeds inside Serenity as they climaxed at the same time. Breathing heavily, he slowly pulled himself from her. Walking over to one of the boxes that set in the corner of their large bathroom, he opened one and pulled out two towels, wetting them both before handing one to Serenity. After cleaning themselves, they both walked back out to the U-Haul, making several trips as they brought all the boxes inside. Reason, feeling hungry, opened the Door Dash app and placed an order from his favorite Mexican restaurant, ordering a platter of street tacos for the two of them to share.

"I'm about to go to the liquor store. I'ma need a drink if I'ma get through all these damn boxes," Reason spoke, looking around the living room. "We need to make our first toast anyway."

"Cool, if you gonna get some liquor, make sure you get a chaser."

Reason kissed Serenity before grabbing his key fob and walking out the house. He smiled, knowing that everything in his life had finally worked out for the good. There was a point in his life that he hated waking up in the morning. Now, he woke up each morning, excited to have another day to show his love to Serenity. She'd really come into his life and showed him that true love really did exist. She showed him why he went through the heartbreak. Everything that Reason had gone through had led him straight to Serenity, and there was no place else he would rather be.

Serenity had walked in his life and had given him Heaven on Earth. For that, he would be eternally grateful. For years, he'd thought Kalahni was the love of his life, his soul mate. However, now that he'd met the woman that God had truly made for him, he now knew that nothing he ever thought was love had come close to what Serenity gave him.

***

"You still want to go to Walmart and Home Depot today?" Reason asked, placing the boxes he'd just brought in on the floor in the living room.

Serenity looked around the room at all the boxes that needed to be unpacked. The U-Haul was still half full of boxes that needed to be brought inside.

"Nah, we can just go tomorrow."

Nodding his head, Reason went back out to the U-Haul to gather more boxes. Serenity grabbed the boxes that were labeled cleaning supplies and made her way to the kitchen. She began cleaning the kitchen from top to bottom, making sure every speck of dust was gone. When she was done, she began putting away all the dishes in the spots she'd chosen for them to go.

"We gotta go to Walmart tonight either way. I don't know where the air mattress is that I bought. Our bed not coming until tomorrow, so we need something to sleep on tonight. I ain't fuckin' up my back sleeping on these hard ass floors."

"Yeah, I ain't with that either. Let me just finish putting up these glasses and we can go after that."

"Cool, let me know when you ready."

About fifteen minutes later, Reason and Serenity were on their way to Walmart. Serenity turned on her playlist, and Ella Mai's *Little Things* began to play. She looked at Reason, smiling at him before she began singing the lyrics. "Hang your coat, take off your shoes, hot water in the tub for you."

"You better stop rubbin' on me and singing before I pull this car over and give you all this dick," Reason joked.

"Boy, shut up. You so silly."

Pulling into the parking lot of Walmart, they parked before walking inside. Serenity grabbed a cart, pushing it around the store as they gathered everything they needed. About two hours later, they were done and heading back home.

"I'll bring everything in if you wanna get back to putting away the dishes," Reason suggested.

"Yeah, that's cool with me. It's gonna take us forever to put all this shit away, and I was thinking that maybe we should just do some decal stickers and LED lights for the kids' rooms instead of painting. That will save us a lot of time if we want to have their rooms set up by the time they get back Sunday night."

"See, what would I do without you? That is a great idea." Reason began getting the bags from the car as Serenity walked inside and went straight to the kitchen. Reason walked up to their room and inflated the air mattress before placing sheets, covers, and pillows onto it. Once he was finished, he walked into the bathroom, running hot water into their brand new jacuzzi tub before placing bubble bath into it. He lit several candles around the bathroom before turning off all the lights and walking back downstairs.

"Come here, baby. I got something to show you upstairs," Reason encouraged, walking into the kitchen, taking her hand.

"Okay, one second. I just got one more box of dishes to put up before I move to the pots and pans."

"That shit ain't going nowhere. We can do that later. What I have to show you is very important."

Serenity obliged, walking out the kitchen with Reason leading the way. They walked into the candlelit bathroom, and Serenity smiled as she looked up at him.

"Aww, babe, you ran us a bubble bath? That was sweet." She kissed Reason's lips softly before taking off her clothes and stepping into the bubbly water.

Reason's manhood insanity stiffened at the sight of her toned body. Removing his clothing, he walked over to the tub. He stepped inside the warm water, easing down into the deep tub. Serenity leaned back against his chest as Reason wrapped his arms around her, holding her tightly. Serenity loved the way Reason's hands felt on her skin, and she melted into him as he hugged her tighter. The joy she felt when she was with him was unmatched, and she couldn't wait to see what the future held for the two of them.

"We need to take baths together like this more often. I like this," Reason deduced, kissing Serenity on her cheek.

"Yeah, we do. This is nice. I'm gonna get us a bath shelf, so we can sit my laptop on it and watch a movie next time we take a bath."

"Yeah, that's a dope idea. Movie nights in the tub."

They sat in the tub, cuddling, until the water turned cold. When they were done, they both stepped out the tub before stepping into their separate rain shower. Reason finished washing off before Serenity did, so he stepped out the shower first. He wrapped a towel around his waist and walked into the master bedroom.

Serenity turned off the shower, stepping out and drying off before wrapping the towel around her body. She walked into their bedroom and almost passed out when she saw Reason looking up at her. He was shirtless but had on a pair of gray sweatpants. He was down on one knee, holding a small, black, velvet box in his hand.

"Reason, what is this?" Serenity asked, smiling from ear to ear. She walked up to him slowly, and he took her hand.

"Serenity Jones, I want you to know that you have made me the happiest man in the world. The light you have shined on my life has guided me out of my darkest situations. You make me better. I thrive to be better because I know you deserve the best version of me. I want to spend the rest of my life showing you how grateful I am to have you here. Serenity, would you do me the honor of being my wife and spending your life with me?"

"Oh, my God, Reason. Yes, baby! Yes, I'll marry you."

Serenity got on her knees as well, wrapping her arms around Reason and hugging him tightly as joy filled her. Tears fell from her eyes as Reason slid the three-carat diamond ring on her finger.

"Wait, so this means we like engaged?" Serenity asked, holding her hand up, admiring her ring.

"That's right, baby. Yo ass stuck with me now. I don't know what you gon' do now," Reason joked.

Serenity's heart was warm. They love she felt for this man, her man, was unlike anything she'd ever felt before. She was convinced that this was what love felt like when you finally found the person that was meant for you. Every heartache and setback had led her to this moment, her rainbow after the storm. Because of Reason, Serenity now had her own testimony of love, something that needed to go down in history as the greatest love story ever told. This was something she couldn't wait to sit around the living room and tell her grandchildren — the story of the time she healed the heart of a Detroit gangsta.

The End!

Other Books By

URBAN AINT DEAD

Tales 4rm Da Dale

The Hottest Summer Ever

Hittin' Licks For The Holidays: Atlanta

Wet Dreams On Lockdown: The Nurse

How To Publish A Book From Prison

How To Invest In The Stock Market From Prison

By **Elijah R. Freeman**

Despite The Odds

By **Juhnell Morgan**

Good Girls Gone Rogue

Good Girls Gone Rogue 2

By **Manny Black**

Hittaz

Hittaz 2

Hittaz 3

Hittaz 4

Hittaz 5

Hittaz 6

Coldhearted

Coldhearted 2

Coldhearted 3

By **Lou Garden Price, Sr.**

Charge It To The Game

Charge It To The Game 2

Charge It To The Game 3

A Summer To Remember With My Hitta

Snatched Up By A Hitta

Santa Sent Me A Real One For Christmas

Wet Dreams On Lockdown: The Unit Manager

Thug Me The Right Way 2

Thug Me The Right Way 3

Seizing A Gangsta's Heart For The Summer

Yours For The Taking

Wrapped Up In A Hitta's Love For Christmas

By **Nai**

A Set Up For Revenge

A Set Up For Revenge 2

Wet Dreams On Lockdown: The Librarian

By **Ashley Williams**

Trickin' On A Heaux For Christmas

Homie Hoppin' For The Holidays

Wet Dreams On Lockdown: The Female C.O

Letters Of His Love

By **Telia Teanna**

The State's Witness

The State's Witness 2

The State's Witness 3

This Time Won't You Save Me

This Time Won't You Save Me 2

His Summer Side Piece

A Holiday Heist
By **Kyiris Ashley**

Stuck In The Trenches
Stuck In The Trenches 2
By **Huff Tha Great**

Melted The Heart Of A Menace
Wet Dreams On Lockdown: Lieutenant Grace
By **P. Wise**

Merry Trapmas
By **Mia Sky**

Thug Me The Right Way
By **DiamondATL & Nai**

Wet Dreams On Lockdown: The Counselor
By **Paris Iman**

Wet Dreams On Lockdown: The Male C.O
By **Tamyra Griffin**

Wet Dreams On Lockdown: The Captain
By **TN Jones**

Wet Dreams On Lockdown: The Warden
By **Shawnice**

Atlantastan
Atlantastan 2
By **Chris Green**

IN The Streetz

IN The Streetz 2

IN The Streetz 3

IN The Streetz 4

By **Tron Hill**

Hittin' Licks For The Holidays: New York

By **Freshh Moneyy**

Coming Soon From
URBAN AINT DEAD

The Hottest Summer Ever 2
THE G-CODE
Tales 4rm Da Dale 2
How To Build Your Credit From Prison
By **Elijah R. Freeman**

Good Girls Gone Rogue 3
By **Manny Black**

Despite The Odds 2
By **Juhnell Morgan**

Foreva Your Gangsta
By **Nai**

This Time Won't You Save Me 3
By **Kyiris Ashley**

Atlantastan 3
By **Chris Green**

IN The Streetz 5
By **Tron Hill**